Ghosts of Christmas Past

Edited with an introduction by
TIM MARTIN

JOHN MURRAY

First published in paperback in Great Britain in 2017
by John Murray (Publishers)
An Hachette UK Company

1

Introduction © Tim Martin 2017
Selection copyright © John Murray (Publishers) 2017

A CIP catalogue record for this title is available from the British Library

ISBN 978-1-47366-346-6
Ebook ISBN 978-1-47366-347-3

Typeset in Adobe Garamond by
Palimpsest Book Production Ltd, Falkirk, Stirlingshire

Printed and bound in Great Britain by Clays Ltd, St Ives plc

John Murray policy is to use papers that are natural, renewable and
recyclable products and made from wood grown in sustainable forests.
The logging and manufacturing processes are expected to conform
to the environmental regulations of the country of origin.

John Murray (Publishers)
Carmelite House
50 Victoria Embankment
London EC4Y 0DZ

www.johnmurray.co.uk

Contents

Introduction

We may think of ghost stories as a Victorian tradition, but the habit of telling spooky tales at the end of the year goes back a long way. Centuries before Dickens and his contemporaries began writing for a mass market fascinated by spiritualism and the occult, workers and families were gathering in the long nights to work, talk and swap tall stories of magic and horror. In 1725 the Newcastle historian Henry Bourne noted that 'nothing is commoner in country places than for a whole family in a winter's evening, to sit round the fire, and tell stories of apparitions and ghosts'. Even further back in time is Shakespeare's character Mamilius, who observes that 'a sad tale's best for winter: I have one/Of sprites and goblins'. In the trough of the seasons, where the days wither and the nights stretch out, our old nocturnal anxieties start to prickle again – and there has always been a delicious *Schadenfreude* about the ghost story, with its implicit contrast between Them Out There (hag-ridden, bedevilled, plagued by horrors) and Us In Here by the fire with our friends.

Despite the title, this isn't entirely a book of Christmas ghost stories. The spooky tale set at Christmas, as opposed to *told at* Christmas, turns out to be less common than one might think – and one stricture feels like enough for a collection. Accordingly, and because misrule is another Christmas tradition, the wandering spirits that throng this collection haven't had their IDs checked very carefully. Some are ghosts of Christmas past. Others are half-glimpsed Christmas monsters, horrifying Christmas presentiments, amorphous pools of Christmas malevolence, Christmas drunken hallucinations and, in one case, what may well be a Christmas demon. All, however, confine their haunting, chasing, shambling or manifesting to the festive season.

Ghost stories, appropriately, are a moonlighter's profession: even the big names rarely build entire careers on them. M. R. James, whose Christmas chiller *The Story of a Disappearance and an Appearance* is one of his most frightening pieces, was a medieval historian, director of the Fitzwilliam and translator of the Apocrypha who wrote (and read) his ghost stories to make friends shiver by candlelight. Edith Nesbit, who appears here with the elusive and terrifying *The Shadow*, fitted hers in between bestselling children's novels (*The Railway Children, The Phoenix and the Carpet*) and running the Fabian Society. Writers as austere and waspish as Muriel Spark jostle in these pages with those as foppish and jolly as Jerome K. Jerome; in her bewilderingly calm ghost story *The Leaf-Sweeper* the ghost is still alive, in his Christmas entertainment (*The Ghost of the Blue Chamber*) the phantom likes to tempt boozers and strangle carol-singers. Like many such collections, this one is a strange come-all-ye of authors, like a hobbyist's convention or the cast list for an Agatha Christie mystery.

'You must have noticed,' runs a line in Nesbit's *The Shadow*, 'that all the real ghost stories you have ever come close to, are like this . . . no explanation, no logical coherence'. Literary ghost stories, however, tend to split into two camps: the haunting and the horrifying. Robert Aickman's *The Visiting Star*, like all this inimitably peculiar writer's work, is more Tales of the Cryptic than Tales from the Crypt as it weaves its theatrical Christmas nightmare out of stifled comedy, semi-obscure mythical allusions (Iblis and Myrrha, among others, are worth scurrying to the encyclopaedia for) and moments of heart-stopping dread. In *The Vanishing House*, by the forgotten Victorian writer Bernard Capes, a bunch of travelling musicians encounter a winter horror in a brief dialect story that starts out as broad and boozy comedy and ends up feeling like a lost fragment of folktale. The yachtsman Frank Cowper's *Christmas Eve on a Haunted Hulk*, a story disconcertingly cast in the documentary tone of real experience, is choked with ambient dread – few ghost stories manage to make *sound* so terrifying – but similarly light on explanation and dramatic form.

Other stories train their sights on emotions more complex than terror. Jenn Ashworth's clever, despairing *Dinner for One*, not the only story in this volume to be narrated by the ghost, casts its central haunting as a ghastly co-dependent relationship or a form of domestic abuse. Louis de Bernières's *My Beautiful House* is an oddity: a supernatural story, told with an admirable lightness of touch, that turns out to be more interested in heart-tugging melancholy than in bald horror. Kelly Link's rather wondrous *The Lady and the Fox*, meanwhile, mixes timeworn notions of Christmas ghostery with a crackling contemporary tone and a fantasy story as old (and everlastingly youthful) as Tam Lin himself.

Not all the revenants here are quite so subtle. Neil Gaiman's *Nicholas Was*, written for a Christmas card, is a 100-word exercise in jet-black comedy, describing a seasonal favourite who is less St Nicholas than Old Nick. *Someone in the Lift* by L. P. Hartley (famous for *The*

Go-Between, but a dedicated producer of supernatural stories as well) is a *Twilight Zone*-style shocker whose nastiness is almost too blatant – that dot-dot-dot ending! – but manages a genuinely unsettling tone of supernatural foreshadowing in the first part. Written with dreadful relish, E. F. Benson's *The Step* may be the least subtle of the stories in this collection: it's a tale that demands to be read aloud, with the kind of climactic 'boo' that should send listeners howling into the festive night.

And what a long night it is, out there beyond the warm rooms and the firelight. Don't worry about the noises. Ignore the moving shapes. It's time to step out. Turn the page. Oh, and happy Christmas. If you come back.

*The Story of a Disappearance
and an Appearance*

M. R. JAMES

The letters which I now publish were sent to me recently by a person who knows me to be interested in ghost stories. There is no doubt about their authenticity. The paper on which they are written, the ink, and the whole external aspect put their date beyond the reach of question.

The only point which they do not make clear is the identity of the writer. He signs with initials only, and as none of the envelopes of the letters are preserved, the surname of his correspondent – obviously a married brother – is as obscure as his own. No further preliminary explanation is needed, I think. Luckily the first letter supplies all that could be expected.

~

Letter I

GREAT CHRISHALL, Dec. 22, 1837.

MY DEAR ROBERT,—It is with great regret for the enjoyment I am losing, and for a reason which you will deplore equally with myself, that I write to inform you that I am unable to join your circle for this Christmas: but you will agree with me that it is unavoidable when I say that I have within these few hours received a letter from Mrs. Hunt at B——, to the effect that our Uncle Henry has suddenly and mysteriously disappeared, and begging me to go down there immediately and join the search that is being made for him. Little as I, or you either, I think, have ever seen of Uncle, I naturally feel that this is not a request that can be regarded lightly, and accordingly I propose to go to B—— by this afternoon's mail, reaching it late in the evening. I shall not go to the Rectory, but put up at the King's Head, and to which you may address letters. I enclose a small draft, which you will please make use of for the benefit of the young people. I shall write you daily (supposing me to be detained more than a single day) what goes on, and you may be sure, should the business be cleared up in time to permit of my coming to the Manor after all, I shall present myself. I have but a few minutes at disposal. With cordial greetings to you all, and many regrets, believe me, your affectionate Bro.,

W. R.

~

Letter II

KING'S HEAD, Dec. 23, '37.

MY DEAR ROBERT,—In the first place, there is as yet no news of Uncle H., and I think you may finally dismiss any idea – I won't say hope – that I might after all 'turn up' for Xmas. However, my thoughts will be with you, and you have my best wishes for a really festive day. Mind that none of my nephews or nieces expend any fraction of their guineas on presents for me.

Since I got here I have been blaming myself for taking this affair of Uncle H. too easily. From what people here say, I gather that there is very little hope that he can still be alive; but whether it is accident or design that carried him off I cannot judge. The facts are these. On Friday the 19th, he went as usual shortly before five o'clock to read evening prayers at the Church; and when they were over the clerk brought him a message, in response to which he set off to pay a visit to a sick person at an outlying cottage the better part of two miles away. He paid the visit, and started on his return journey at about half-past six. This is the last that is known of him. The people here are very much grieved at his loss; he had been here many years, as you know, and though, as you also know, he was not the most genial of men, and had more than a little of the martinet in his composition, he seems to have been active in good works, and unsparing of trouble to himself.

Poor Mrs. Hunt, who has been his housekeeper ever since she left Woodley, is quite overcome: it seems like the end of the world to her. I am glad that I did not entertain the idea of taking quarters at the Rectory; and I have declined several kindly offers of hospitality from people in the place, preferring as I do to be independent, and finding myself very comfortable here.

You will, of course, wish to know what has been done in the way of inquiry and search. First, nothing was to be expected from investigation at the Rectory; and to be brief, nothing has transpired. I asked Mrs. Hunt – as others had done before – whether there was either any unfavourable symptom in her master such as might portend a sudden stroke, or attack of illness, or whether he had ever had reason to apprehend any such thing: but both she, and also his medical man, were clear that this was not the case. He was quite in his usual health. In the second place, naturally, ponds and streams have been dragged, and fields in the neighbourhood which he is known to have visited last, have been searched – without result. I have myself talked to the parish clerk and – more important – have been to the house where he paid his visit.

There can be no question of any foul play on these people's part. The one man in the house is ill in bed and very weak: the wife and the children of course could do nothing themselves, nor is there the shadow of a probability that they or any of them should have agreed to decoy poor Uncle H. out in order that he might be attacked on the way back. They had told what they knew to several other inquirers already, but the woman repeated it to me. The Rector was looking just as usual: he wasn't very long with the sick man – 'He ain't,' she said, 'like some what has a gift in prayer; but there, if we was all that way, 'owever would the chapel people get their living?' He left some money when he went away, and one of the children saw him cross the stile into the next field. He was dressed as he always was: wore his bands – I gather he is nearly the last man remaining who does so – at any rate in this district.

You see I am putting down everything. The fact is that I have nothing else to do, having brought no business papers with me; and, moreover, it serves to clear my own mind, and may suggest points which have been overlooked. So I shall continue to write all that passes, even to conversations if need be – you may read or not as you please, but pray keep the letters. I have another reason for writing so fully, but it is not a very tangible one.

You may ask if I have myself made any search in the fields near the cottage. Something – a good deal – has been done by others, as I mentioned; but I hope to go over the ground tomorrow. Bow Street has now been informed, and will send down by tonight's coach, but I do not think they will make much of the job. There is no snow, which might have helped us. The fields are all grass. Of course I was on the qui vive for any indication today both going and returning; but there was a thick mist on the way back, and I was not in trim for wandering about unknown pastures, especially on an evening when bushes looked like men, and a cow lowing in the distance might have been the last trump. I assure you, if Uncle Henry had stepped out from among the trees in a little copse which borders the path at one place, carrying his head under his arm, I should have been very little more uncomfortable than I was. To tell you the truth, I was rather expecting something of the kind. But I must drop my pen for the moment: Mr. Lucas, the curate, is announced.

Later. Mr. Lucas has been, and gone, and there is not much beyond the decencies of ordinary senti-ment to be got from him. I can see that he has given up any idea that the Rector can be alive, and that, so far as he can be, he is truly sorry. I can also discern that even in a more emotional person than Mr. Lucas, Uncle Henry was not likely to inspire strong attachment.

Besides Mr. Lucas, I have had another visitor in the shape of my Boniface – mine host of the 'King's Head' – who came to see whether I had everything I wished, and who really requires the pen of a Boz to do him justice. He was very solemn and weighty at first. 'Well, sir,' he said, 'I suppose we must bow our 'ead beneath the blow, as my poor wife had used to say. So far as I can gather there's been neither hide nor yet hair of our late respected incumbent scented out as yet; not that he was what the Scripture terms a hairy man in any sense of the word.'

I said – as well as I could – that I supposed not, but could not help adding that I had heard he was sometimes a little difficult to deal with. Mr. Bowman looked at me sharply for a moment, and then passed in a flash from solemn sympathy to impassioned declamation. 'When I think,' he said, 'of the language that man see fit to employ to me in this here parlour over no more a matter than a cask of beer – such a thing as I told him might happen any day of the week to a man with a family – though as it turned out he was quite under a mistake, and that I knew at the time, only I was that shocked to hear him I couldn't lay my tongue to the right expression.'

He stopped abruptly and eyed me with some embarrassment. I only said, 'Dear me, I'm sorry to hear you had any little differences; I suppose my uncle will be a good deal missed in the parish?' Mr. Bowman drew a long breath. 'Ah, yes!' he said; 'your uncle! You'll understand me when I say that for the moment it had slipped my remembrance that he was a relative; and natural enough, I must say, as it should, for as to you bearing any resemblance to – to him, the notion of any such a thing is clean ridiculous. All the same, 'ad I 'ave bore it in my mind, you'll be among the first to feel, I'm sure, as I should have abstained my lips, or rather I should not have abstained my lips with no such reflections.'

I assured him that I quite understood, and was going to have asked him some further questions, but he was called away to see after some business. By the way, you need not take it into your head that he has anything to fear from the inquiry into poor Uncle Henry's disappearance – though, no doubt, in the watches of the night it will occur to him that I think he has, and I may expect explanations tomorrow.

I must close this letter: it has to go by the late coach.

~

Letter III

Dec. 25, '37.

MY DEAR ROBERT,—This is a curious letter to be writing on Christmas Day, and yet after all there is nothing much in it. Or there may be – you shall be the judge. At least, nothing decisive. The Bow Street men practically say that they have no clue.

The length of time and the weather conditions have made all tracks so faint as to be quite useless: nothing that belonged to the dead man – I'm afraid no other word will do – has been picked up.

As I expected, Mr. Bowman was uneasy in his mind this morning; quite early I heard him holding forth in a very distinct voice – purposely so, I thought – to the Bow Street officers in the bar, as to the loss that the town had sustained in their Rector, and as to the necessity of leaving no stone unturned (he was very great on this phrase) in order to come at the truth. I suspect him of being an orator of repute at convivial meetings.

When I was at breakfast he came to wait on me, and took an opportunity when handing a muffin to say in a low tone, 'I 'ope, sir, you reconize as my feelings towards your relative is not actuated by any taint of what you may call melignity – you can leave the room, Eliza, I will see the gentleman 'as all he requires with my own hands – I ask your pardon, sir, but you must be well aware a man is not always master of himself: and when that man has been 'urt in his mind by the application of expressions which I will go so far as to say 'ad not ought to have been made use of (his voice was rising all this time and his face growing redder); no, sir; and 'ere, if you will permit of it, I should like to explain to you in a very few words the exact state of the bone of contention. This cask – I might more truly call it a firkin – of beer—'

I felt it was time to interpose, and said that I did not see that it would help us very much to go into that matter in detail. Mr. Bowman acquiesced, and resumed more calmly:

'Well, sir, I bow to your ruling, and as you say, be that here or be it there, it don't contribute a great deal, perhaps, to the present question. All I wish you to understand is that I am prepared as you are yourself to lend every hand to the business we have afore us, and – as I took the opportunity to say as much to the Orficers not three-quarters of an hour ago – to leave no stone unturned as may throw even a spark of light on this painful matter.'

In fact, Mr. Bowman did accompany us on our exploration, but though I am sure his genuine wish was to be helpful, I am afraid he did not contribute to the serious side of it. He appeared to be under the impression that we were likely to meet either Uncle Henry or the person responsible for his disappearance, walking about the fields – and did a great deal of shading his eyes with his hand and calling our attention, by pointing with his stick, to distant cattle and labourers. He held several long conversations with old women whom we met, and was very strict and severe in his manner – but on each occasion returned to our party saying, 'Well, I find she don't seem to 'ave no connexion with this sad affair. I think you may take it from me, sir, as there's little or no light to be looked for from that quarter; not without she's keeping somethink back intentional.'

We gained no appreciable result, as I told you at starting; the Bow Street men have left the town, whether for London or not, I am not sure.

This evening I had company in the shape of a bagman, a smartish fellow. He knew what was going forward, but though he has been on the roads for some days about here, he had nothing to tell of suspicious characters – tramps, wandering sailors or gipsies. He was very full of a capital Punch and Judy Show he had seen this same day at W——, and asked if it had been here yet, and advised me by no means to miss it if it does come. The best Punch and the best Toby dog, he said, he had ever come across. Toby dogs, you know, are the last new thing in the shows. I have only seen one myself, but before long all the men will have them.

Now why, you will want to know, do I trouble to write all this to you? I am obliged to do it, because it has something to do with another absurd trifle (as you will inevitably say), which in my present state of rather unquiet fancy – nothing more, perhaps – I have to put down. It is a dream, sir, which I am going to record, and I must say it is one of the oddest I have had. Is there anything in it beyond what the bagman's talk and Uncle Henry's disappearance could have suggested? You, I repeat, shall judge: I am not in a sufficiently cool and judicial frame to do so.

It began with what I can only describe as a pulling aside of curtains: and I found myself seated in a place – I don't know whether indoors or out. There were people – only a few – on either side of me, but I did not recognize them, or indeed think much about them. They never spoke, but, so far as I remember, were all grave and pale-faced and looked fixedly before them. Facing me there was a Punch and Judy Show, perhaps rather larger than the ordinary ones, painted with black figures on a reddish-yellow ground. Behind it and on each side was only darkness, but in front there was a sufficiency of light. I was 'strung up' to a high degree of expectation and listened every moment to hear the panpipes and the Roo-too-too-it. Instead of that there came suddenly an enormous – I can use no other word – an enormous single toll of a bell, I don't know from how far off – somewhere behind. The little curtain flew up and the drama began.

I believe someone once tried to re-write Punch as a serious tragedy; but whoever he may have been, this performance would have suited him exactly. There was something Satanic about the hero. He varied his methods of attack: for some of his victims he lay in wait, and to see his horrible face – it was yellowish white, I may remark – peering round the wings made me think of the Vampyre in Fuseli's foul sketch. To others he was polite and carneying – particularly to the unfortunate alien who can only say Shallabalah – though what Punch said I never could catch. But with all of them I came to dread the moment of death. The crack of the stick on their skulls, which in the ordinary way delights me, had here a crushing sound as if the bone was giving way, and the victims quivered and kicked as they lay. The baby – it sounds more ridiculous as I go on – the baby, I am sure, was alive. Punch wrung its neck, and if the choke or squeak which it gave were not real, I know nothing of reality.

The stage got perceptibly darker as each crime was consummated, and at last there was one murder which was done quite in the dark, so that I could see nothing of the victim, and took some time to effect. It was accompanied by hard breathing and horrid muffled sounds, and after it Punch came and sat on the foot-board and fanned himself and looked at his shoes, which were bloody, and hung his head on one side, and sniggered in so deadly a fashion that I saw some of those beside me cover their faces, and I would gladly have done the same. But in the meantime the scene behind Punch was clearing, and showed, not the usual house front, but something more ambitious – a grove of trees and the gentle slope of a hill, with a very natural – in fact, I should say a real – moon shining on it. Over this there rose slowly an object which I soon perceived to be a human figure with something peculiar about the head – what, I was unable at first to see. It did not stand on its feet, but began creeping or dragging itself across the middle distance towards Punch, who still sat back to it; and by this time, I may remark (though it did not occur to me at the moment) that all pretence of this being a puppet show had vanished. Punch was still Punch, it is true, but, like the others, was in some sense a live creature, and both moved themselves at their own will.

When I next glanced at him he was sitting in malignant reflection; but in another instant some-thing seemed to attract his attention, and he first sat up sharply and then turned round, and evidently caught sight of the person that was approaching him and was in fact now very near. Then, indeed, did he show unmistakable signs of terror: catching up his stick, he rushed towards the wood, only just eluding the arm of his pursuer, which was suddenly flung out to intercept him. It was with a revulsion which I cannot easily express that I now saw more or less clearly what this pursuer was like. He was a sturdy figure clad in black, and, as I thought, wearing bands: his head was covered with a whitish bag.

The chase which now began lasted I do not know how long, now among the trees, now along the slope of the field, sometimes both figures disappearing wholly for a few seconds, and only some uncertain sounds letting one know that they were still afoot. At length there came a moment when Punch, evidently exhausted, staggered in from the left and threw himself down among the trees. His pursuer was not long after him, and came looking uncertainly from side to side. Then, catching sight of the figure on the ground, he too threw himself down – his back was turned to the audience – with a swift motion twitched the covering from his head, and thrust his face into that of Punch. Everything on the instant grew dark.

There was one long, loud, shuddering scream, and I awoke to find myself looking straight into the face of – what in all the world do you think? – but a large owl, which was seated on my window-sill immediately opposite my bed-foot, holding up its wings like two shrouded arms. I caught the fierce glance of its yellow eyes, and then it was gone. I heard the single enormous bell again – very likely, as you are saying to yourself, the church clock; but I do not think so – and then I was broad awake.

All this, I may say, happened within the last half-hour. There was no probability of my getting to sleep again, so I got up, put on clothes enough to keep me warm, and am writing this rigmarole in the first hours of Christmas Day. Have I left out anything? Yes, there was no Toby dog, and the names over the front of the Punch and Judy booth were Kidman and Gallop, which were certainly not what the bagman told me to look out for.

By this time, I feel a little more as if I could sleep, so this shall be sealed and wafered.

~

Letter IV

Dec. 26, '37.

MY DEAR ROBERT,—All is over. The body has been found. I do not make excuses for not having sent off my news by last night's mail, for the simple reason that I was incapable of putting pen to paper. The events that attended the discovery bewildered me so completely that I needed what I could get of a night's rest to enable me to face the situation at all. Now I can give you my journal of the day, certainly the strangest Christmas Day that ever I spent or am likely to spend.

The first incident was not very serious. Mr. Bowman had, I think, been keeping Christmas Eve, and was a little inclined to be captious: at least, he was not on foot very early, and to judge from what I could hear, neither men or maids could do anything to please him. The latter were certainly reduced to tears; nor am I sure that Mr. Bowman succeeded in preserving a manly composure. At any rate, when I came downstairs, it was in a broken voice that he wished me the compliments of the season, and a little later on, when he paid his visit of ceremony at breakfast, he was far from cheerful: even Byronic, I might almost say, in his outlook on life.

'I don't know,' he said, 'if you think with me, sir; but every Christmas as comes round the world seems a hollerer thing to me. Why, take an example now from what lays under my own eye. There's my servant Eliza – been with me now for going on fifteen years. I thought I could have placed my confidence in Eliza, and yet this very morning – Christmas morning too, of all the blessed days in the year – with the bells a ringing and – and – all like that – I say, this very morning, had it not have been for Providence watching over us all, that girl would have put – indeed I may go so far to say, 'ad put the cheese on your breakfast table—' He saw I was about to speak, and waved his hand at me. 'It's all very well for you to say, "Yes, Mr. Bowman, but you took away the cheese and locked it up in the cupboard," which I did, and have the key here, or if not the actual key one very much about the same size. That's true enough, sir, but what do you think is the effect of that action on me? Why it's no exaggeration for me to say that the ground is cut from under my feet. And yet when I said as much to Eliza, not nasty, mind you, but just firm like, what was my return? "Oh," she says: "Well," she says, "there wasn't no bones broke, I suppose." Well, sir, it 'urt me, that's all I can say: it 'urt me, and I don't like to think of it now.'

There was an ominous pause here, in which I ventured to say something like, 'Yes, very trying,' and then asked at what hour the church service was to be. 'Eleven o'clock,' Mr. Bowman said with a heavy sigh. 'Ah, you won't have no such discourse from poor Mr. Lucas as what you would have done from our late Rector. Him and me may have had our little differences, and did do, more's the pity.'

I could see that a powerful effort was needed to keep him off the vexed question of the cask of beer, but he made it. 'But I will say this, that a better preacher, nor yet one to stand faster by his rights, or what he considered to be his rights – however, that's not the question now – I for one, never set under. Some might say, "Was he a eloquent man?" and to that my answer would be: "Well, there you've a better right per'aps to speak of your own uncle than what I have." Others might ask, "Did he keep a hold of his congregation?" and there again I should reply, "That depends." But as I say—Yes, Eliza, my girl, I'm coming—eleven o'clock, sir, and you inquire for the King's Head pew.' I believe Eliza had been very near the door, and shall consider it in my vail.

The next episode was church: I felt Mr. Lucas had a difficult task in doing justice to Christmas sentiments, and also to the feeling of disquiet and regret which, whatever Mr. Bowman might say, was clearly prevalent. I do not think he rose to the occasion. I was uncomfortable. The organ wolved

– you know what I mean: the wind died – twice in the Christmas Hymn, and the tenor bell, I suppose owing to some negligence on the part of the ringers, kept sounding faintly about once in a minute during the sermon. The clerk sent up a man to see to it, but he seemed unable to do much. I was glad when it was over. There was an odd incident, too, before the service. I went in rather early, and came upon two men carrying the parish bier back to its place under the tower. From what I overheard them saying, it appeared that it had been put out by mistake, by some one who was not there. I also saw the clerk busy folding up a moth-eaten velvet pall – not a sight for Christmas Day.

I dined soon after this, and then, feeling disinclined to go out, took my seat by the fire in the parlour, with the last number of Pickwick, which I had been saving up for some days. I thought I could be sure of keeping awake over this, but I turned out as bad as our friend Smith. I suppose it was half-past two when I was roused by a piercing whistle and laughing and talking voices outside in the market-place. It was a Punch and Judy – I had no doubt the one that my bagman had seen at W———. I was half delighted, half not – the latter because my unpleasant dream came back to me so vividly;

but, anyhow, I determined to see it through, and I sent Eliza out with a crown-piece to the performers and a request that they would face my window if they could manage it.

The show was a very smart new one; the names of the proprietors, I need hardly tell you, were Italian, Foresta and Calpigi. The Toby dog was there, as I had been led to expect. All B—— turned out, but did not obstruct my view, for I was at the large first-floor window and not ten yards away.

The play began on the stroke of a quarter to three by the church clock. Certainly it was very good; and I was soon relieved to find that the disgust my dream had given me for Punch's onslaughts on his ill-starred visitors was only transient. I laughed at the demise of the Turncock, the Foreigner, the Beadle, and even the baby. The only drawback was the Toby dog's developing a tendency to howl in the wrong place. Something had occurred, I suppose, to upset him, and something considerable: for, I forget exactly at what point, he gave a most lamentable cry, leapt off the foot-board, and shot away across the market-place and down a side street. There was a stage-wait, but only a brief one. I suppose the men decided that it was no good going after him, and that he was likely to turn up again at night.

We went on. Punch dealt faithfully with Judy, and in fact with all comers; and then came the moment when the gallows was erected, and the great scene with Mr. Ketch was to be enacted. It was now that something happened of which I can certainly not yet see the import fully. You have witnessed an execution, and know what the criminal's head looks like with the cap on. If you are like me, you never wish to think of it again, and I do not willingly remind you of it. It was just such a head as that, that I, from my somewhat higher post, saw in the inside of the show-box; but at first the audience did not see it. I expected it to emerge into their view, but instead of that there slowly rose for a few seconds an uncovered face, with an expression of terror upon it, of which I have never imagined the like. It seemed as if the man, whoever he was, was being forcibly lifted, with his arms somehow pinioned or held back, towards the little gibbet on the stage. I could just see the nightcapped head behind him. Then there was a cry and a crash. The whole show-box fell over backwards; kicking legs were seen among the ruins, and then two figures – as some said; I can only answer for one – were visible running at top speed across the square and disappearing in a lane which leads to the fields.

Of course everybody gave chase. I followed; but the pace was killing, and very few were in, literally, at the death. It happened in a chalk pit: the man went over the edge quite blindly and broke his neck. They searched everywhere for the other, until it occurred to me to ask whether he had ever left the market-place. At first everyone was sure that he had; but when we came to look, he was there, under the show-box, dead too.

But in the chalk pit it was that poor Uncle Henry's body was found, with a sack over the head, the throat horribly mangled. It was a peaked corner of the sack sticking out of the soil that attracted attention. I cannot bring myself to write in greater detail.

I forgot to say the men's real names were Kidman and Gallop. I feel sure I have heard them, but no one here seems to know anything about them.

I am coming to you as soon as I can after the funeral. I must tell you when we meet what I think of it all.

Dinner for One

JENN ASHWORTH

She – Maggie, that is – comes in from the field. She rinses her hands at the sink and without removing her muddy shoes nor taking off her coat, sits at the table and stares at the steaming cup waiting for her. It's as if she's never seen it before: her trembling fingers hover over her lips until the tea is quite cold. She sweeps it onto the floor. The cup shatters and tea runs along the tiles. Now she goes out, picking her way across the overgrown garden, over the broken fence at the far end, and off, into the musty field where the pylons are and the wild hares run and fight and fuck.

Maggie has not been herself lately. She spends hours walking aimlessly in the field, picking up broken and jagged pieces of rock: the remnants of a dry stone wall long since dissolved and returned to the elements. She brings them back to the garden. She will not explain why. She barely eats, has not washed in days and is changing her clothes only rarely. While she does not seem to enjoy staying in the cottage, she does not appear to want to be out of sight of it. She always stays in view of one of the windows, either in the garden, or the field, or pacing up and down the misty lane. As if she is looking for something. Today she gathers stones for several hours. When she returns it is dark and there's a fresh cup of tea waiting for her. She ignores it completely and climbs the stairs, slamming the doors. She smells of soil but then again, so do I.

My patience is starting to wear thin. I'm the one who isn't sleeping, who can drift off only for a few moments at a time before being roused by nightmares (the smell of earth, shouting, a great pain; a remembered argument of some kind, perhaps). Sometimes, time itself seems to slip out of place. One minute I am looking out at the electricity sub-station in the field beyond the garden, the dark pylons and lines faded and murky in the mist, and at Maggie, picking her way over the uneven ground, head down. If I close my eyes for even a moment, the light will change, the mist will lift or deepen, the shadows on the ground will whirl jaggedly into a different direction entirely. Things tend to move around me. I know how that sounds, but there is a pile of newspapers over there on the kitchen table that simply wasn't there a moment ago. The plants on the windowsill seem to have grown inches in the space of one afternoon.

I am not sure what is causing it. Maggie herself appears to enjoy rearranging things in the kitchen cupboards just for the sake of it. Boxes of eggs and loaves of bread disappear. The curtains open and close, open and close, and I never see her doing it. The cushions on the sofa aren't arranged in the way I like them – the way I taught her when we first moved into the cottage. I have tried to speak to her but as I said she is not herself and of the two of us I have always needed to be the rock. So I clear the cup and saucer away. Return the kitchen cupboards to a state of order, everything where it should be.

When I go up to her she is lying on our bed, staring at the ceiling. The place is disgusting – she hasn't cleaned properly in months.

Leave it all to me. I'll do everything.

I tell her that it will be better if it is just the two of us for Christmas lunch this year. No family or friends to disturb, to ask questions, to express misplaced concern. No special events, just a good, home-cooked meal and our own company. We can bolt the door, light a fire and keep the world outside at bay, where it belongs.

Then we have a silly argument. She turns on the

television in the bedroom while I am speaking. It's rude – anyone would agree – and so I turn it off. She turns it back on again. Love can make you childish and we carry on like this – on, off, on off – some variety performance with comedians and musicians each doing a turn in a crowded auditorium – until she gets bored and gives up. She sits quietly on the edge of the bed in the dark.

Passion can look like this sometimes, I tell her.

Maggie is the kind of woman who needs to be told things many times, in different ways, before an important piece of information will really sink in. I am a patient person. It's why we are so well suited.

We are made for each other.

I keep telling her. I won't give up on her.

That is what love means.

She is weeping softly, her hands over her face.

~

The next day is just the same and her mood has not improved. It might be something to do with the lack of sunlight. The cottage is shrouded in a constant fog. The air feels heavy and wet. It smells like soil and mould and rotting leaves and I develop a cough, my breathing laboured. It becomes difficult for me to shake the impression there is something in my lungs – some spore or mould caused by lack of exercise and the dank air. I tell her we need a holiday. Somewhere dry and hot, for the sake of our health. There's been no snow here yet but the sky is low and grey and she is still ignoring me.

Come on. You're being silly.

We both seem to have lost our appetites. She generally puts on weight during the winter – all those casseroles and dumplings and treacle puddings and roast dinners. It's always something we've needed to address in the spring. But this year, things are different. She looks pale and drawn, like some kind of wraith. When most people are slowing down, enjoying evenings spent under a blanket in front of a black and white film with a hot chocolate or even a brandy to keep them company, Maggie is running buckets of hot water and bleach and scrubbing at imaginary stains on the kitchen floor.

I am not without sympathy. Despite my own condition, I cook little things for her, trying to tempt her appetite – bowls of soup and toasted sandwiches, pieces of fish from the freezer, chicken breasts in rich sauces. I lay the table and light candles. I bring out the best cutlery and the crystal glasses. She will touch nothing, but only regards the carefully arranged dishes and steaming plates with an unreadable look on her face.

I suppose this is the silent treatment. To punish me for that silly business with the television. It's childish of her and she knows it gets to me. Because of her I sweep all the plates and dishes off the table. They roll and shatter on the kitchen floor. She doesn't move. I throw the candlesticks into the sink, and lift the bubbling pans from the cooker and hold them over my head.

You need to stop this now, Maggie.

I don't mean to threaten her but it all gets too much for me sometimes. I am working so hard, and sleeping so little. Can't she see what she is doing to me? How cruel she is being? I can't stop coughing. It feels like there's something caught in my throat but nothing comes up, no matter how hard I try. She should not push my buttons like this.

~

Our nearest neighbours are half a mile away down the lane. We've always taken pains to avoid them but today they come to the house and bring a covered dish that smells like some kind of meat. Along with that, a bunch of flowers and a box of chocolates.

We're worried about you.

Maggie won't let them in and the woman hands over the food at the door. The man plucks leaves from the hedge and eyes the neglected flowerbeds.

You will let me know if you need anything doing? Anything fetching or carrying? He laughs. *I'm your man.*

When they leave I am so overcome by jealousy I slam every door in the house. She gets into bed with her boots on and pulls the duvet over her ears. The meat sits on the kitchen table until it grows a skin of blue and yellow mould and finally, she throws it out.

~

The phone rings. She answers it in the hallway and sits at the bottom of the stairs, twisting the cord around her fingers until the tips of them turn blue.

No news yet.

Sweat gathers on her top lip and between her eyebrows. She's getting spots. I put some of her medicated cream on the shopping list: she won't think of it herself.

No, nothing at all. There's been no sign.

I don't like her hiding herself away to speak on the phone. We agreed that it wasn't right to talk about our relationship with others, not even her mother. Everyone goes through a rough spot now and again. It's our business and no one else's. A truly committed couple shouldn't have secrets from one another. I turn the hallway light on and off to get her attention – to remind her about the peak rate charges. The lights flash and the unopened letters and takeaway flyers on the doormat swirl around the room in a paper snowstorm and I keep at it until she remembers our agreement and hangs up.

I think I'm going mad, she says, looking at the air between us.

I embrace her but she only shivers and pulls away to turn all the radiators in the house onto their highest setting. I wait for her in our bedroom, worrying about my cough and my breath, which is starting to smell like mushrooms, even to myself. She will not come up, but begins again to scrub the kitchen floor.

~

The structure – if that's the right word for it – that she is making in the garden from her collection of stones is growing. It started as a clumsy-looking rockery, made of grey, mossy and lichen-spotted rocks she'd dragged back from the field. She has made no attempt to obtain plants nor to install a water feature and the rest of the garden is as poorly kept as it ever was. I used to mow that lawn but now I can only watch as the grass becomes shaggy and clogged with moss and she angrily, obsessively, piles up her stolen stones and slots them together, building up the tower until it reaches her knees, her hips, her waist. Beyond the fence, the hares chatter and scurry, wearing desire paths in the dew-clotted grass of the field.

We need to decide what you want to do about Christmas. Goose this year? Or ham?

She doesn't respond. Someone knocks at the door. We chose this place for its privacy – few people want to live within the crackling aura of the sub-station. She looks around her in such a state of wide-eyed shock that it is almost comic. She waits. She is kneeling in the kitchen, her bucket of water at her elbow. We paid a fortune for that floor – it is Welsh slate – a shade of greyish blue exactly the same colour as a newborn's eyes. You drop anything onto that floor and it breaks – butterfingers Maggie learned *that* the first time she dropped my favourite dish while she was washing up. She's more careful now, but this is ridiculous. How many times have I seen her wash the floor this past few weeks? She ignores the doorbell and continues to scrub.

You could eat your dinner off it, I tell her, and turn out the lights to let her know it's time for bed. She won't come. She lies awake on the couch until dawn.

~

The day comes. Traditionally Christmas is a time for far-flung relatives to reunite around a turkey and for every waif and stray to find a place at a friend's table. But this year, I want it to be just us. We've gone off track recently. We need a special occasion.

I turn on the taps in the bathroom for her so the room fills with steam. The mirror clouds over and I write my name on it and unwrap her favourite soap. I open all her drawers and pull out her best clothes – she can tidy up later – I want to find that special top I bought for her – there it is – the electric blue one. I drape it on the end of the bed and wait for her to get ready.

Maggie?

She used to take such care of her appearance. She didn't have a natural eye for the colours and styles that suited her the best and she'd sometimes make little errors of judgement and draw too much attention to herself. Once she started letting me advise her in that area, she made improvements quickly. She's let things slide, but I should have guided her more.

It's ready, love. Come out of the bath now.

I wait at the table for what seems like hours. She doesn't come. I can't eat. It feels, sometimes, like my limbs are frozen, my mouth filled with earth. It is time for her to stop being so selfish and start to think about me for a change. She can't have things her own way all the time. Does she think she'll be able to carry on like this when there are children to look after? There's a tin of soup on the counter and I am sure it wasn't there a moment ago. The dishes cool. I left her to buy the pudding, to choose the wine and cheese. She's said, in the past, that I'm too controlling. That I don't let her make decisions. So I've given her an opportunity to contribute to our meal. To put her own stamp on things. It'll be a little test for her. Let's see what she makes of it.

She doesn't come. There are foxes in the garden again, screaming.

~

The doorbell rings. This time, whoever it is won't be dissuaded and when there's no answer, he or she moves around the side of the house, bangs at the back door, and again, at the kitchen window. Maggie is kneeling on the floor with her bucket of bleach and water and her scrubbing brush – the place is spotless and her hands are red raw – and she looks up. They see her and she stands, wiping her hands on her jeans.

They come in through the back door. One of them talks about the progression of some report or complaint that has been made – it's hard to keep up with the intricacies of the conversation – and the other pretends to be paying attention, but is looking at the wet puddle on the kitchen floor, the bucket of cooling water, the scrubbing brush. She never used to be this house-proud. I want to tell them that but it seems disloyal. Maggie is speaking.

I don't know where he is. I keep telling you. It's been four months now. Since before Christmas.

The people that are sitting in her kitchen start asking her about me – about my finances – my bank statements. There have been no withdrawals from my account, they say, in months. Would there have been, does she think, an account that she didn't know about? A way for me to get my hands on cash, somehow? Eventually they leave.

She leans against the door, breathing heavily. Her legs are shaking. My temper quite overtakes me and I throw the tea-cups into the air, open the cupboards and begin throwing things at her – out of date tins of tuna, a box of instant porridge, the rest of the blue and white tea-cups, a bowl of sugar. The contents of the kitchen whirl and clatter around her. I open the cutlery drawer and the forks and spoons fly across the kitchen in a hail of glittering stainless steel, and still – even after all this – she does not look at me. Her hands are over her face and she is screaming. A broken bottle of olive oil seeps into the slate floor. We bought that in Greece and it cost a fortune. The kitchen smells like a taverna now and she can scrub all she likes but she will never, ever get that dark stain out of those slates.

Leave me in peace, she says. *Can't you, even now, just leave me in peace?*

The two visitors are picking their way along the path through the daffodils in the grass and they were, I think, about to turn the corner and make their way to their car, when they stop, and look over their shoulders. Maggie stands at the sink amid the ruins of the kitchen, watching them.

She whimpers.

Go back. Go back to your car.

One of them stops and nudges, with the polished toe of his boot, the pile of stones that Maggie has been working on. It looks like one of those cairns you see in the Lake District sometimes, and entirely out of keeping with the style of the cottage and the landscape it is set in. The cairn – if that's what it is – seems to interest him. Maggie drops to her knees in the ruin of the kitchen, glass crunching under her boots. She finds her brush and starts on the floor again, ignoring the debris, the broken crockery and spilled packets of food, the oil soaking into everything. She is frantic and keening under her breath.

Go away. Go away, go away. Go away.

There was a time when domestic disagreements stayed private. When a couple would be left to sort out their issues in their own way. The man kicks at the cairn again, covering his nose and mouth with his hand, and the stones shift and tumble and Maggie cries out, rubbing hopelessly at the dark stain on the kitchen floor and sobbing as the pair retrace their footsteps and return to our cottage.

The Shadow

E. NESBIT

This is not an artistically rounded-off ghost story, and nothing is explained in it, and there seems to be no reason why any of it should have happened. But that is no reason why it should not be told. You must have noticed that all the real ghost stories you have ever come close to, are like this in these respects – no explanation, no logical coherence. Here is the story.

There were three of us and another, but she had fainted suddenly at the second extra of the Christmas dance, and had been put to bed in the dressing room next to the room which we three shared. It had been one of those jolly, old-fashioned dances where nearly everybody stays the night, and the big country house is stretched to its utmost containing – guests harbouring on sofas, couches, settles, and even mattresses on floors. Some of the young men actually, I believe, slept on the great dining table. We had talked of our partners, as girls will, and then the stillness of the manor house, broken only by the whisper of the wind in the cedar branches, and the scraping of their harsh fingers against our window panes, had pricked us to such a luxurious confidence in our surroundings of bright chintz and candle flame and fire light, that we had dared to talk of ghosts – in which, we all said, we did not believe one bit. We had told the story of the phantom coach, and the horribly strange bed, and the lady in the sacque, and the house in Berkeley Square.

We none of us believed in ghosts, but my heart, at least, seemed to leap to my throat and choke me there, when a tap came to our door – a tap faint, not to be mistaken.

'Who's there?' said the youngest of us, craning a lean neck towards the door. It opened slowly, and I give you my word, the instant of suspense that followed is still reckoned among my life's least confident moments. Almost at once the door opened fully, and Miss Eastwich, my aunt's housekeeper, companion and general stand-by looked in on us.

We all said 'Come in,' but she stood there. She was, at all normal hours, the most silent woman I have ever known. She stood and looked at us, and shivered a little. So did we – for in those days corridors were not warmed by hot-water pipes, and the air from the door was keen.

'I saw your light,' she said at last, 'and I thought it was late for you to be up – after all this gaiety. I thought perhaps—' her glance turned towards the door of the dressing room.

'No,' I said, 'she's fast asleep.' I should have added a goodnight, but the youngest of us forestalled my speech. She did not know Miss Eastwich as we others did; did not know how her persistent silence had built a wall round her – a wall that no one dared to break down with the commonplaces of talk, or the littlenesses of mere human relationship. Miss Eastwich's silence had taught us to treat her as a machine; and as other than a machine we never dreamed of treating her. But the youngest of us had seen Miss Eastwich for the first time that day. She was young, crude, ill-balanced, subject to blind, calf-like impulses. She was also the heiress of a rich tallow-chandler, but that has nothing to do with this part of the story. She jumped up from the hearth rug, her unsuitably rich silk lace-trimmed dressing gown falling back from her thin collarbones, and ran to the door and put an arm round Miss Eastwich's prim, lisse-encircled neck. I gasped. I should as soon have dared to embrace Cleopatra's Needle. 'Come in,' said the youngest of us – 'come in and get warm. There's lots of cocoa left.' She drew Miss Eastwich in and shut the door.

The vivid light of pleasure in the housekeeper's pale

eyes went through my heart like a knife. It would have been so easy to put an arm round her neck, if one had only thought she wanted an arm there. But it was not I who had thought that – and indeed, my arm might not have brought the light evoked by the thin arm of the youngest of us.

'Now,' the youngest went on eagerly, 'you shall have the very biggest, nicest chair, and the cocoapot's here on the hob as hot as hot – and we've all been telling ghost stories, only we don't believe in them a bit; and when you get warm you ought to tell one too.'

Miss Eastwich – that model of decorum and decently done duties, tell a ghost story!

'You're sure I'm not in your way,' Miss Eastwich said, stretching her hands to the blaze. I wondered whether housekeepers have fires in their rooms even at Christmas time. 'Not a bit' – I said it, and I hope I said it as warmly as I felt it. 'I – Miss Eastwich – I'd have asked you to come in other times – only I didn't think you'd care for girls' chatter.'

The third girl, who was really of no account, and that's why I have not said anything about her before, poured cocoa for our guest. I put my fleecy Madeira shawl round her shoulders. I could not think of anything else to do for her, and I found myself wishing desperately to do something. The smiles she gave us were quite pretty. People can smile prettily at forty or fifty, or even later, though girls don't realise this. It occurred to me, and this was another knife-thrust, that I had never seen Miss Eastwich smile – a real smile – before. The pale smiles of dutiful acquiescence were not of the same blood as this dimpling, happy, transfiguring look.

'This is very pleasant,' she said, and it seemed to me that I had never before heard her real voice. It did not please me to think that at the cost of cocoa, a fire, and my arm round her neck, I might have heard this new voice any time these six years.

'We've been telling ghost stories,' I said. 'The worst of it is, we don't believe in ghosts. No one has ever seen one.'

'It's always what somebody told somebody, who told somebody you know,' said the youngest of us, 'and you can't believe that, can you?'

'What the soldier said is not evidence,' said Miss Eastwich. Will it be believed that the little Dickens quotation pierced one more keenly than the new smile or the new voice?

'And all the ghost stories are so beautifully rounded off – a murder committed on the spot – or a hidden treasure, or a warning . . . I think that makes them harder to believe. The most horrid ghost story I ever heard was one that was quite silly.'

'Tell it.'

'I can't – it doesn't sound anything to tell. Miss Eastwich ought to tell one.'

'Oh do,' said the youngest of us, and her salt cellars loomed dark, as she stretched her neck eagerly and laid an entreating arm on our guest's knee.

'The only thing that I ever knew of was – was hearsay,' she said slowly, 'till just the end.'

I knew she would tell her story, and I knew she had never before told it, and I knew she was only telling it now because she was proud, and this seemed the only way to pay for the fire and the cocoa, and the laying of that arm round her neck.

'Don't tell it,' I said suddenly. 'I know you'd rather not.'

'I daresay it would bore you,' she said meekly, and the youngest of us, who, after all, did not understand everything, glared resentfully at me.

'We should just *love* it,' she said. '*Do* tell us. Never mind if it isn't a real, proper, fixed-up story. I'm certain anything *you* think ghostly would be quite too beautifully horrid for anything.'

Miss Eastwich finished her cocoa and reached up to set the cup on the mantelpiece.

'It can't do any harm,' she said half to herself, 'they don't believe in ghosts, and it wasn't exactly a ghost either. And they're all over twenty – they're not babies.'

There was a breathing time of hush and expectancy. The fire crackled and the gas suddenly glared higher because the billiard lights had been put out. We heard the steps and voices of the men going along the corridors.

'It is really hardly worth telling,' Miss Eastwich said doubtfully, shading her faded face from the fire with her thin hand.

We all said 'Go on – oh, go on – do!'

'Well,' she said, 'twenty years ago – and more than that – I had two friends, and I loved them more than anything in the world. And they married each other—'

She paused, and I knew just in what way she had loved each of them. The youngest of us said:

'How awfully nice for you. Do go on.'

She patted the youngest's shoulder, and I was glad that I had understood, and that the youngest of all hadn't. She went on.

'Well, after they were married, I did not see much of them for a year or two; and then he wrote and asked me to come and stay, because his wife was ill, and I should cheer her up, and cheer him up as well; for it was a gloomy house, and he himself was growing gloomy too.'

I knew, as she spoke, that she had every line of that letter by heart.

'Well, I went. The address was in Lee, near London; in those days there were streets and streets of new villa-houses growing up round old brick mansions standing in their own grounds, with red walls round, you know, and a sort of flavour of coaching days, and post chaises, and Blackheath highwaymen about them. He had said the house was gloomy, and it was called "The Firs", and I imagined my cab going through a dark, winding shrubbery, and drawing up in front of one of these sedate, old, square houses. Instead, we drew up in front of a large, smart villa, with iron railings, gay encaustic tiles leading from the iron gate to the stained-glass-panelled door, and for shrubbery only a few stunted cypresses and aucubas in the tiny front garden. But inside it was all warm and welcoming. He met me at the door.'

She was gazing into the fire, and I knew she had forgotten us. But the youngest girl of all still thought it was to us she was telling her story.

'He met me at the door,' she said again, 'and thanked me for coming, and asked me to forgive the past.'

'What past?' said that high priestess of the *inápropos*, the youngest of all.

'Oh – I suppose he meant because they hadn't invited me before, or something,' said Miss Eastwich worriedly, 'but it's a very dull story, I find, after all, and—'

'Do go on,' I said – then I kicked the youngest of us, and got up to rearrange Miss Eastwich's shawl, and said in blatant dumb show, over the shawled shoulder: 'Shut up, you little idiot—'

After another silence, the housekeeper's new voice went on.

'They were very glad to see me, and I was very glad to be there. You girls, now, have such troops of friends, but these two were all I had – all I had ever had. Mabel wasn't exactly ill, only weak and excitable. I thought he seemed more ill than she did. She went to bed early and before she went, she asked me to keep him company through his last pipe, so we went into the dining room and sat in the two armchairs on each side of the fireplace. They were covered with green leather, I remember. There were bronze groups of horses and a black marble clock on the mantelpiece – all wedding presents. He poured out some whisky for himself, but he hardly touched it. He sat looking into the fire. At last I said:

"What's wrong? Mabel looks as well as you could expect."

'He said, "Yes – but I don't know from one day to another that she won't begin to notice something wrong. That's why I wanted you to come. You were always so sensible and strong-minded, and Mabel's like a little bird on a flower."

'I said yes, of course, and waited for him to go on.

I thought he must be in debt, or in trouble of some sort. So I just waited. Presently he said:

"'Margaret, this is a very peculiar house—" he always called me Margaret. You see we'd been such old friends. I told him I thought the house was very pretty, and fresh, and homelike – only a little too new – but that fault would mend with time. He said:

"'It is new: that's just it. We're the first people who've ever lived in it. If it were an old house, Margaret, I should think it was haunted."

'I asked if he had seen anything. "No," he said "not yet."

"'Heard, then?" said I.

"'No – not heard either," he said, "but there's a sort of feeling: I can't describe it – I've seen nothing and I've heard nothing, but I've been so near to seeing and hearing, just near, that's all. And something follows me about – only when I turn round, there's never anything, only my shadow. And I always feel that I *shall* see the thing next minute – but I never do – not quite – it's always just not visible."

'I thought he'd been working rather hard – and tried to cheer him up by making light of all this. It was just nerves, I said. Then he said he had thought I could help him, and did I think anyone he had wronged could have laid a curse on him, and did I believe in curses. I said I didn't – and the only person anyone could have said he had wronged forgave him freely, I knew, if there was anything to forgive. So I told him this too.'

It was I, not the youngest of us, who knew the name of that person, wronged and forgiving.

'So then I said he ought to take Mabel away from the house and have a complete change. But he said No; Mabel had got everything in order, and he could never manage to get her away just now without explaining everything – "and, above all," he said, "she mustn't guess there's anything wrong. I daresay I shan't feel quite such a lunatic now you're here."

'So we said goodnight.'

'Is that all the story?' said the third girl, striving to convey that even as it stood it was a good story.

'That's only the beginning,' said Miss Eastwich. 'Whenever I was alone with him, he used to tell me the same thing over and over again, and at first when I began to notice things, I tried to think that it was his talk that had upset my nerves. The odd thing was that it wasn't only at night – but in broad daylight – and particularly on the stairs and passages. On the staircase the feeling used to be so awful that I have had to bite my lips till they bled to keep myself from running upstairs at full speed. Only I knew if I did I should go mad at the top. There was always something behind me – exactly as he had said – something that one could just not see. And a sound that one could just not hear. There was a long corridor at the top of the house. I have sometimes almost seen something – you know how one sees things without looking – but if I turned round, it seemed as if the thing drooped and melted into my shadow. There was a little window at the end of the corridor.

'Downstairs there was another corridor, something like it, with a cupboard at one end and the kitchen at the other. One night I went down into the kitchen to heat some milk for Mabel. The servants had gone to bed. As I stood by the fire, waiting for the milk to boil, I glanced through the open door and along the passage. I never could keep my eyes on what I was doing in that house. The cupboard door was partly open; they used to keep empty boxes and things in it. And, as I looked, I knew that now it was not going to be "almost" any more. Yet I said, "Mabel?" not because I thought it could be Mabel who was crouching down there, half in and half out of the cupboard. The thing was grey at first, and then it was black. And when I whispered, "Mabel," it seemed to sink down till it lay like a pool of ink on the floor, and then its edges drew in, and it seemed to flow, like ink when you tilt up the paper you have spilt it on; and it flowed into the cupboard till it was all gathered into the shadow there. I saw it go quite plainly. The gas was full on in the kitchen. I screamed aloud, but even then, I'm thankful to say, I had enough sense to upset the boiling milk, so that when he came downstairs three steps at a time, I had the excuse for my scream of a scalded hand. The explanation satisfied Mabel, but next night he said:

"'Why didn't you tell me? It was that cupboard. All the horror of the house comes out of that. Tell me – have you seen anything yet? Or is it only the nearly seeing and nearly hearing still?"

'I said, "You must tell me first what you've seen." He told me, and his eyes wandered, as he spoke, to the shadows by the curtains, and I turned up all three gas lights, and lit the candles on the mantelpiece. Then we looked at each other and said we were both mad, and thanked God that Mabel at least was sane. For what he had seen was what I had seen.

'After that I hated to be alone with a shadow, because at any moment I might see something that would crouch, and sink, and lie like a black pool, and then slowly draw itself into the shadow that was nearest. Often that shadow was my own. The thing came first at night, but afterwards there was no hour safe from it. I saw it at dawn and at noon, in the dusk and in the firelight, and always it crouched and sank, and was a pool that flowed into some shadow and became part of it. And always I saw it with a straining of the eyes – a pricking and aching. It seemed as though I could only just see it, as if my sight, to see it, had to be strained to the uttermost. And still the sound was in the house – the sound that I could just not hear. At last, one morning early, I did hear it. It was close behind me, and it was only a sigh. It was worse than the thing that crept into the shadows.

'I don't know how I bore it. I couldn't have borne it, if I hadn't been so fond of them both. But I knew in my heart that, if he had no one to whom he could speak openly, he would go mad, or tell Mabel. His was not a very strong character; very sweet, and kind, and gentle, but not strong. He was always easily led. So I stayed on and bore up, and we were very cheerful, and made little jokes, and tried to be amusing when Mabel was with us. But when we were alone, we did not try to be amusing. And sometimes a day or two would go by without our seeing or hearing anything, and we should perhaps have fancied that we had fancied what we had seen and heard – only there was always the feeling of there being something about the house, that one could just not hear and not see. Sometimes we used to try not to talk about it, but generally we talked of nothing else at all. And the weeks went by, and Mabel's baby was born. The nurse and the doctor said that both mother and child were doing well. He and I sat late in the dining room that night. We had neither of us seen or heard anything for three days; our anxiety about Mabel was lessened. We talked of the future – it seemed then so much brighter than the past. We arranged that, the moment she was fit to be moved, he should take her away to the sea, and I should superintend the moving of their furniture into the new house he had already chosen. He was gayer than I had seen him since his marriage – almost like his old self. When I said goodnight to him, he said a lot of things about my having been a comfort to them both. I hadn't done anything much, of course, but still I am glad he said them.

'Then I went upstairs, almost for the first time without the feeling of something following me. I listened at Mabel's door. Everything was quiet. I went on towards my own room, and in an instant I felt that there was something behind me. I turned. It was crouching there; it sank, and the black fluidness of it seemed to be sucked under the door of Mabel's room.

'I went back. I opened the door a listening inch. All was still. And then I heard a sigh close behind me. I opened the door and went in. The nurse and the baby were asleep. Mabel was asleep too – she looked so pretty – like a tired child – the baby was cuddled up into one of her arms with its tiny head against her side. I prayed then that Mabel might never know the terrors that he and I had known. That those little ears might never hear any but pretty sounds, those clear eyes never see any but pretty sights. I did not dare to pray for a long time after that. Because my prayer was answered. She never saw, she never heard anything more in this world. And now I could do nothing more for him or for her.

'When they had put her in her coffin, I lighted wax candles round her, and laid the horrible white flowers that people will send near her, and then I saw he had followed me. I took his hand to lead him away.

'At the door we both turned. It seemed to us that we heard a sigh. He would have sprung to her side, in I don't know what mad, glad hope. But at that instant we both saw it. Between us and the coffin, first grey, then black, it crouched an instant, then sank and liquefied – and was gathered together and drawn till it ran into the nearest shadow. And the nearest shadow was the shadow of Mabel's coffin. I left the next day. His mother came. She had never liked me.'

Miss Eastwich paused. I think she had quite forgotten us.

'Didn't you see him again?' asked the youngest of us all.

'Only once,' Miss Eastwich answered, 'and something black crouched then between him and me. But it was only his second wife, crying beside his coffin. It's not a cheerful story is it? And it doesn't lead anywhere. I've never told anyone else. I think it was seeing his daughter that brought it all back.'

She looked towards the dressing-room door.

'Mabel's baby?'

'Yes – and exactly like Mabel, only with his eyes.'

The youngest of all had Miss Eastwich's hands, and was petting them.

Suddenly the woman wrenched her hands away, and stood at her gaunt height, her hands clenched, eyes straining. She was looking at something that we could not see, and I know what the man in the Bible meant when he said: 'The hair of my flesh stood up.'

What she saw seemed not quite to reach the height of the dressing-room door handle. Her eyes followed it down, down – widening and widening. Mine followed them – all the nerves of them seemed strained to the uttermost – and I almost saw – or did I quite see? I can't be certain. But we all heard the long-drawn, quivering sigh. And to each of us it seemed to be breathed just behind us.

It was I who caught up the candle – it dripped all over my trembling hand – and was dragged by Miss Eastwich to the girl who had fainted during the second extra. But it was the youngest of all whose lean arms were round the housekeeper when we turned away, and that have been round her many a time since, in the new home where she keeps house for the youngest of us.

The doctor who came in the morning said that Mabel's daughter had died of heart disease – which she had inherited from her mother. It was that that had made her faint during the second extra. But I have sometimes wondered whether she may not have inherited something from her father. I have never been able to forget the look on her dead face.

This Beautiful House

LOUIS DE BERNIÈRES

I love it at Christmas. I just sit here at the end of the garden on top of the rockery, like a garden gnome. I don't find the stones uncomfortable. I sit here and look at the house. It's very beautiful, I always did think so. I grew up here, and I am still here now, although I spend much of my time out in the garden just looking.

Other people may not think it beautiful, but it's beautiful to me mainly because I always loved it. I loved my childhood in this house, and I loved it when I had to go abroad on military service, because it represented everything I was fighting for, and I loved it when I came back to Notwithstanding from Korea, and settled into the life I was born to. Here is the clump of bamboos behind which I used to conceal myself when playing hide and seek with my brothers and sister. Further up there on the left is a bird table that I made when I was at school. It's amazing that it hasn't rotted away by now. The lawn isn't very smooth, there's too much couch grass, but we used to set up a putting green on it in the summer, and it ruined my father's scores at the real golf course because he kept hitting the ball a long way past the hole. Here is the big apple tree that was so easy to climb, and produced great Bramleys that my mother made into pies. One year we tried to make cider, but it was very sharp. We had rabbits in the orchard, in a big wire enclosure that was movable. They kept the grass mown if you remembered to move the cage around. Of course they'd escape quite often by burrowing underneath, and they'd go and raid the vegetable patch, but they came when you called them anyway. The cage started life as a chicken run, but we found them too ill-natured. There used to be a modest fruit cage just here as well, and I often had to go into it to free the robins and blackbirds that got stuck inside. They would fly about in a silly panic, and didn't know you were trying to be helpful. 'Funny kind of fruit cage,' my father used to say. 'Keeps birds in instead of out.'

The house isn't very old. It's Edwardian, and it's made of nice red brick with tiles coming half way down the walls, in the Surrey farmhouse style. I remember when the Virginia creeper and the wisteria were planted, and now they're all over the walls. I don't know who the architect was, but it's a very conventional design. Most of the other family houses around here are quite similar. The first people to live here came down from the North. I think they were in textiles. Then it belonged to a writer who was quite famous in his time, but now no one's even heard of him. Then it belonged to a retired naval officer and his wife, and then it was ours. I have so many happy memories. I don't ever want to leave.

Inside there were about five bedrooms. My parents had the one at the back. Mine was above the kitchen. Every morning the smell of frying eggs and sausages would get me out of bed in a good mood. My room wasn't big, but it was big enough for my model aeroplanes to hang from the ceiling on string, and for my toy soldiers to have decent-sized battles. I had a little cannon that worked on a spring, and you could put ball-bearings or matches into it, pull back the lever, release it, and mow down the troops. When I grew up I would find little ball-bearings all over the place.

My brother Michael shared a room with my other brother Sebastian. They were twins, but not identical. My sister Catherine had the room opposite my parents, and sometimes I would creep into her room at night with a sheet over my head, and give her a fright, or I'd listen for when she went to the loo, and I'd lie down at the corner of the corridor and grab her ankle as she went past in the dark. It worked every time. Then my mother told me to stop doing it, because it was unnerving being woken up by screaming in the middle of the night. Catherine used to get revenge by leaning over the banisters of the landing, and spitting on my head when I was underneath in the hallway. It's hard to imagine that she grew up to be so beautiful and refined, and married a baronet.

On the top floor up the back stairs, under the roof, is a lovely big dusty attic. I think it had been fitted out for a servant to live in, because it had a proper little fireplace, and the rafters were all boarded in. I spent hours up there. I fixed a dartboard to the wall, and I threw darts at it, backhand, underarm, over my shoulder, every possible way. I got very good at it. It was one of my party tricks. I used to go up there when I was miserable as well, because no one would know I was weeping.

I always liked the bells. You'd press a button on the wall in any room, and it would ring in the pantry, and a little brown semaphore would wave back and forth in a box above the door, and indicate which room you were ringing from. Catherine and I used to push the buttons to make my mother go to the front door and find nobody there. Once we did it, and my mother went to the door, and when she opened it, the cat was sitting there on the mat in the porch, looking up at her as if he'd pressed it himself. The cat just walked past her into the hallway, and my mother was astonished for a short time, until she realised that it couldn't possibly have been Tobermory that rang the bell. Tobermory was named after a talking cat in a story that my father read to us once. The moral of the story was that if you can talk, it's better not to tell the truth.

Our phone number was 293, amazing when you consider how long the numbers are nowadays.

I love sitting here at Christmas time, at the end of the garden. I don't feel the cold. I like to sit here because the house looks so wonderful with the Christmas tree behind the French windows. There's a full moon, and I can see everything around me with perfect clarity. The stars are out, and I can never remember which ones are the planets. Perhaps they're the very bright ones. Sebastian used to point them out to me, but I don't know how he knew. I used to point them out to girlfriends when I was being romantic, but I was bluffing. I knew that they didn't know either. The house and the garden and the sky look like something out of a Christmas card, appropriately enough. The only thing missing is snow. I only ever remember one white Christmas, when it snowed as we came out of church, and Catherine was wearing a lilac coat with a hood that had a lining of white rabbit fur that framed her face and made me think that she was the prettiest sister that anyone ever had. Everything is silver and shadow now, except for the Christmas tree, which is glowing with all sorts of different coloured lights, that reflect off the tinsel and the glass balls.

It reminds me, it can't be helped, of that dreadful night of the fire. We had little candles in those days, little candles that sat on cups that clipped to the branches of the Christmas tree, along with all the tatty taffeta angels that we'd inherited. It looked magical, but it wasn't ever a good idea. The trees dry out, and they're full of resin. They go up like a torch.

We all went to midnight Mass, and when we got home we had a nightcap. We talked about plans for Christmas Day. My father used to like to go shooting, but my mother more or less forbade him. She said it wasn't nice to go round bowling over rabbits and blasting birds out of the sky on the day when our Saviour was born to bring peace and harmony to the world. We decided we'd all walk to Abbot's Notwithstanding and back again before lunch, but my mother would have to drop out because someone had to baste the goose. I think she was probably relieved, because she wasn't a great one for unnecessary exercise.

The whole family were there, including the baronet. We liked the baronet. He didn't put on any airs, and he didn't have any side. He had a quiet charm and a confidence. He gave up the army for Catherine's sake, because she didn't want to have to be sent off all over the world at a moment's notice. It was decent of him because he was a Coldstreamer, he was doing well, and he obviously loved it. He and Catherine came down from Cambridgeshire in the Riley to be with us for Christmas. Sebastian and Michael came down from Merton, and I was living at home anyway, because I'd always loved that house, and didn't want to move anywhere else, not unless I married, and anyway I'd found a decent job in Guildford. I paid rent to my mother without my father knowing, which seemed the best thing. Knowing her, she spent the money on shoes.

That night, what with us being tired and having a tot of whisky inside us, we forgot to put out the candles on the tree, just as anyone might, but the next thing I knew, I woke up choking. I got out of bed, hacking and coughing, and I groped about in the smoke, but I couldn't find the light switch, and there was a terrible pain in my lungs, and I was coughing so much that it was agony. I felt that I was vomiting my lungs up. My eyes stung so badly from the smoke that I couldn't open them, and even so they were still streaming with tears. I remember the pain, the coughing, the stinging in my eyes, and the insuperable fear, the not knowing where I was in the room, the roaring noise, and then it was as if my chest and my brain were full of molten lead, and I must have passed out. I don't really know what happened next.

As I sit here at the end of the garden, on the rockery, looking at the Christmas tree with its electric lights, it's hard to believe that the house was almost gutted. The tree must have set the curtains alight, and so on. Anyway, it's all been repaired, and you'd never know that anything happened. It's part of the wonder of the house. It doesn't die, it just keeps on evolving. The house is alive. It watches over me always, and it's watching me now as I sit here, not feeling the cold, looking at it from the end of the garden.

The house may be alive, but my family aren't. They all perished in the fire, from inhaling the smoke, every one of them, including the cat. Even so, it doesn't stop them turning up. Just now my father put his hand on my shoulder, and said: 'Come on, my boy.' Death hasn't changed him at all. He's just as solid, he's still got the same voice and even the same smell of Three Nuns Navy Cut pipe tobacco. He still smokes a pipe. He wears the plus fours and long socks and brogues that I used to find so embarrassing and old-fashioned. Every time I sit here, he comes and asks me to leave. I wish he wouldn't. I love him, but he isn't entitled to tell me what to do any more.

They're all here now, as solid and real as when they were alive. There's Catherine and her baronet, hand in hand, and Sebastian and Michael looking at me pityingly. There's even the cat. It's not Tobermory. This one is Gerald, and he was two cats later. Gerald used to drink from the dripping tap in the bathroom basin, whereas Tobermory would get under the sofa, stick his claws into the hessian underneath, and drag himself along on his back as fast as he could go. Gerald settles on his haunches and looks up at me with interest, as if I were an experiment.

My mother is here too. She reaches out a hand to try to take mine, and says: 'Please, darling, please,' but I take my hand away, not roughly, but gently. I know she loves me, you see, and I don't want to cause her any hurt. She implores me with her eyes, and still holds out her hand.

'Come on, you big fool,' says Sebastian, grinning like a big schoolboy, and Michael thumps me on the shoulder with the same old fraternal violence, and says: 'Come on, old thing. You've been here quite long enough.'

'I'm watching the house,' I say.

The baronet lights a cigarette, and when he throws the match to the ground, it disappears. 'Look,' he says, 'I know I'm not strictly family and whatnot, only being married in, as it were, but you've got to give it up one of these days, this watching over the house lark.'

'It's really the house watching over me,' I say. 'Anyway, you're all dead.'

'When are you going to understand?' asks Catherine, shaking her head.

'What's wrong with staying here?' I say.

'Please,' says my mother.

After a while they leave, one by one, as they always do. My mother and Catherine give me a gentle kiss on the cheek. It's surprising how you can distinctly feel the kiss of someone who is dead. My father once surprised me by taking my head between his hands and kissing me on the forehead. He would never have done that when he was alive, and he hasn't done it since. Michael and Sebastian subject me to more claps between the shoulder blades. They all turn and wave modestly before they fade away not far from where the bonfire always used to be. Only Gerald stays a little while. He winds himself around my legs a few times, and reaches up to touch a claw to my hand, as he used to when he suspected that it contained a morsel of cheddar cheese. After a while he wanders away after the rest of them.

I don't understand why they keep coming back. I am glad to see them, of course, but they are dead. I keep telling them, but they don't seem to be able to take it in. They don't seem to understand why I won't go with them. Perhaps death makes you less perceptive.

Anyway, I am perfectly contented here, sitting atop this rockery by moonlight, not even feeling the cold, looking at the tree sparkling with so many colours in the French window. I love it here. I love this beautiful house, I love the way it holds me as if it had hands and I was cupped inside them. I sit here and it watches over me, I feel absolute happiness, and there's nothing I'd rather do.

The Leaf-Sweeper

MURIEL SPARK

Behind the town hall there is a wooded parkland which, towards the end of November, begins to draw a thin blue cloud right into itself; and as a rule the park floats in this haze until mid-February. I pass every day, and see Johnnie Geddes in the heart of this mist, sweeping up the leaves. Now and again he stops, and jerking his long head erect, looks indignantly at the pile of leaves, as if it ought not to be there; then he sweeps on. This business of leaf-sweeping he learnt during the years he spent in the asylum; it was the job they always gave him to do; and when he was discharged the town council gave him the leaves to sweep. But the indignant movement of the head comes naturally to him, for this has been one of his habits since he was the most promising and buoyant and vociferous graduate of his year. He looks much older than he is, for it is not quite twenty years ago that Johnnie founded the Society for the Abolition of Christmas.

Johnnie was living with his aunt then. I was at school, and in the Christmas holidays Miss Geddes gave me her nephew's pamphlet, *How to Grow Rich at Christmas*. It sounded very likely, but it turned out that you grow rich at Christmas by doing away with Christmas, and so pondered Johnnie's pamphlet no further.

But it was only his first attempt. He had, within the next three years, founded his society of Abolitionists. His new book, *Abolish Christmas or We Die*, was in great demand at the public library, and my turn for it came at last. Johnnie was really convincing, this time, and most people were completely won over until after they had closed the book. I got an old copy for sixpence the other day, and despite the lapse of time it still proves conclusively that Christmas is a national crime. Johnnie demonstrates that every human-unit in the kingdom faces inevitable starvation within a period inversely proportional to that in which one in every six industrial-productivity units, if you see what he means, stops producing toys to fill the stockings of the educational-intake units. He cites appalling statistics to show that 1.024 per cent of the time squandered each Christmas in reckless shopping and thoughtless churchgoing brings the nation closer to its doom by five years. A few readers protested, but Johnnie was able to demolish their muddled arguments, and meanwhile the Society for the Abolition of Christmas increased. But Johnnie was troubled. Not only did Christmas rage throughout the kingdom as usual that year, but he had private information that many of the Society's members had broken the Oath of Abstention.

He decided, then, to strike at the very roots of Christmas. Johnnie gave up his job on the Drainage Supply Board; he gave up all his prospects, and, financed by a few supporters, retreated for two years to study the roots of Christmas. Then, all jubilant, Johnnie produced his next and last book, in which he established, either that Christmas was an invention of the Early Fathers to propitiate the pagans, or it was invented by the pagans to placate the Early Fathers, I forget which. Against the advice of his friends, Johnnie entitled it *Christmas and Christianity*. It sold eighteen copies. Johnnie never really recovered from this; and it happened, about that time, that the girl he was engaged to, an ardent Abolitionist, sent him a pullover she had knitted, for Christmas; he sent it back, enclosing a copy of the Society's rules, and she sent back the ring. But in any case, during Johnnie's absence, the Society had been undermined by a moderate faction. These moderates finally became more moderate, and the whole thing broke up.

Soon after this, I left the district, and it was some years

before I saw Johnnie again. One Sunday afternoon in summer, I was idling among the crowds who were gathered to hear the speakers at Hyde Park. One little crowd surrounded a man who bore a banner marked 'Crusade against Christmas'; his voice was frightening; it carried an unusually long way. This was Johnnie. A man in the crowd told me Johnnie was there every Sunday, very violent about Christmas, and that he would soon be taken up for insulting language. As I saw in the papers, he was soon taken up for insulting language. And a few months later I heard that poor Johnnie was in a mental home, because he had Christmas on the brain and couldn't stop shouting about it.

After that I forgot all about him until three years ago, in December, I went to live near the town where Johnnie had spent his youth. On the afternoon of Christmas Eve I was walking with a friend, noticing what had changed in my absence, and what hadn't. We passed a long, large house, once famous for its armoury, and I saw that the iron gates were wide open.

'They used to be kept shut,' I said.

'That's an asylum now,' said my friend; 'they let the mild cases work in the grounds, and leave the gates open to give them a feeling of freedom.'

'But,' said my friend, 'they lock everything inside. Door after door. The lift as well; they keep it locked.'

While my friend was chattering, I stood in the gateway and looked in. Just beyond the gate was a great bare elm tree. There I saw a man in brown corduroys, sweeping up the leaves. Poor soul, he was shouting about Christmas.

'That's Johnnie Geddes,' I said. 'Has he been here all these years?'

'Yes,' said my friend as we walked on. 'I believe he gets worse at this time of year.'

'Does his aunt see him?'

'Yes. And she sees nobody else.'

We were, in fact, approaching the house where Miss Geddes lived. I suggested we call on her. I had known her well.

'No fear,' said my friend.

I decided to go in, all the same, and my friend walked on to the town.

Miss Geddes had changed, more than the landscape. She had been a solemn, calm woman, and now she moved about quickly, and gave short agitated smiles. She took me to her sitting-room, and as she opened the door she called to someone inside:

'Johnnie, see who's come to see us!'

A man, dressed in a dark suit, was standing on a chair, fixing holly behind a picture. He jumped down.

'Happy Christmas,' he said. 'A Happy and a Merry Christmas indeed. I do hope,' he said, 'you're going to stay for tea, as we've got a delightful Christmas cake, and at this season of goodwill I would be cheered indeed if you could see how charmingly it's decorated; it has "Happy Christmas" in red icing, and then there's a robin and –'

'Johnnie,' said Miss Geddes, 'you're forgetting the carols.'

'The carols,' he said. He lifted a gramophone record from a pile and put it on. It was 'The Holly and the Ivy'.

'It's "The Holly and the Ivy",' said Miss Geddes. 'Can't we have something else? We had that all morning.'

'It is sublime,' he said, beaming from his chair, and holding up his hand for silence.

While Miss Geddes went to fetch the tea, and he sat absorbed in his carol, I watched him. He was so like Johnnie, that if I hadn't seen poor Johnnie a few moments before, sweeping up the asylum leaves, I would have thought he really was Johnnie. Miss Geddes returned with the tray, and while he rose to put on another record, he said something that startled me.

'I saw you in the crowd that Sunday when I was speaking at Hyde Park.'

'What a memory you have!' said Miss Geddes.

'It must be ten years ago,' he said.

'My nephew has altered his opinion of Christmas,' she explained. 'He always comes home for Christmas now, and don't we have a jolly time, Johnnie?'

'Rather!' he said. 'Oh, let me cut the cake.'

He was very excited about the cake. With a flourish he dug a large knife into the side. The knife slipped, and I saw it run deep into his finger. Miss Geddes did not move. He wrenched his cut finger away, and went on slicing the cake.

'Isn't it bleeding?' I said.

He held up his hand. I could see the deep cut, but there was no blood.

Deliberately, and perhaps desperately, I turned to Miss Geddes.

'That house up the road,' I said, 'I see it's a mental home now. I passed it this afternoon.'

'Johnnie,' said Miss Geddes, as one who knows the game is up, 'go and fetch the mince pies.'

He went, whistling a carol.

'You passed the asylum,' said Miss Geddes wearily.

'Yes,' I said.

'And you saw Johnnie sweeping up the leaves.'

'Yes.'

We could still hear the whistling of the carol.

'Who is *he*?' I said.

'That's Johnnie's ghost,' she said. 'He comes home every Christmas. But,' she said, 'I don't like him. I can't bear him any longer, and I'm going away tomorrow. I don't want Johnnie's ghost, I want Johnnie in flesh and blood.'

I shuddered, thinking of the cut finger that could not bleed. And I left, before Johnnie's ghost returned with the mince pies.

Next day, as I had arranged to join a family who lived in the town, I started walking over about noon. Because of the light mist, I didn't see at first who it was approaching. It was a man, waving his arm to me. It turned out to be Johnnie's ghost.

'Happy Christmas. What do you think,' said Johnnie's ghost, 'my aunt has gone to London. Fancy, on Christmas Day, and I thought she was at church, and here I am without anyone to spend a jolly Christmas with, and, of course, I forgive her, as it's the season of goodwill, but I'm glad to see you, because now I can come with you, wherever it is you're going, and we can all have a Happy . . .'

'Go away,' I said, and walked on.

It sounds hard. But perhaps you don't know how repulsive and loathsome is the ghost of a living man. The ghosts of the dead may be all right, but the ghost of mad Johnnie gave me the creeps.

'Clear off,' I said.

He continued walking beside me. 'As it's the time of goodwill, I make allowances for your tone,' he said. 'But I'm coming.'

We had reached the asylum gates, and there, in the

grounds, I saw Johnnie sweeping the leaves. I suppose it was his way of going on strike, working on Christmas Day. He was making a noise about Christmas.

On a sudden impulse I said to Johnnie's ghost, 'You want company?'

'Certainly,' he replied. 'It's the season of . . .'

'Then you shall have it,' I said.

I stood in the gateway. 'Oh, Johnnie,' I called.

He looked up.

'I've brought your ghost to see you, Johnnie.'

'Well, well,' said Johnnie, advancing to meet his ghost. 'Just imagine it!'

'Happy Christmas,' said Johnnie's ghost.

'Oh, really?' said Johnnie.

I left them to it. And when I looked back, wondering if they would come to blows, I saw that Johnnie's ghost was sweeping the leaves as well. They seemed to be arguing at the same time. But it was still misty, and really, I can't say whether, when I looked a second time, there were two men or one man sweeping the leaves.

Johnnie began to improve in the New Year. At least, he stopped shouting about Christmas, and then he never mentioned it at all; in a few months, when he had almost stopped saying anything, they discharged him.

The town council gave him the leaves of the park to sweep. He seldom speaks, and recognizes nobody. I see him every day at the late end of the year, working within the mist. Sometimes, if there is a sudden gust, he jerks his head up to watch a few leaves falling behind him, as if amazed that they are undeniably there, although, by rights, the falling of leaves should be stopped.

Christmas Eve on a Haunted Hulk

FRANK COWPER

I shall never forget that night as long as I live.

It was during the Christmas vacation 187–. I was staying with an old college friend who had lately been appointed the curate of a country parish, and had asked me to come and cheer him up, since he could not get away at that time.

As we drove along the straight country lane from the little wayside station, it forcibly struck me that a life in such a place must be dreary indeed. I have always been much influenced by local colour; above all things, I am depressed by a dead level, and here was monotony with a vengeance. On each side of the low hedges, lichen-covered and wind-cropped, stretched bare fields, the absolute level of the horizon being only broken at intervals by some mournful tree that pointed like a decrepit fingerpost towards the east, for all its western growth was nipped and blasted by the roaring southwest winds. An occasional black spot, dotted against the grey distance, marked a hayrick or labourer's cottage, while some two miles ahead of us the stunted spire of my friend's church stood out against the wintry sky, amid the withered branches of a few ragged trees. On our right hand stretched dreary wastes of mud, interspersed here and there with firmer patches of land, but desolate and forlorn, cut off from all communication with the mainland by acres of mud and thin streaks of brown water.

A few seabirds were piping over the waste, and this was the only sound, except the grit of our own wheels and the steady step of the horse, which broke the silence.

'Not lively is it?' said Jones; and I couldn't say it was. As we drove 'up street', as the inhabitants fondly called the small array of low houses which bordered the high-road, I noticed the lacklustre expression of the few children and untidy women who were loitering about the doors of their houses.

There was an old tumbledown inn, with a dilapidated signboard, scarcely held up by its rickety ironwork. A daub of yellow and red paint, with a dingy streak of blue, was supposed to represent the Duke's head, although what exalted member of the aristocracy was thus distinguished it would be hard to say. Jones inclined to think it was the Duke of Wellington; but I upheld the theory that it was the Duke of Marlborough, chiefly basing my arguments on the fact that no artist who desired to convey a striking likeness would fail to show the Great Duke in profile, whereas this personage was evidently depicted full face, and wearing a three-cornered hat.

At the end of the village was the church, standing in an untidy churchyard, and opposite it was a neat little house, quite new, and of that utilitarian order of architecture which will stamp the Victorian age as one of the least imaginative of eras. Two windows flanked the front door, and three narrow windows looked out overhead from under a slate roof; variety and distinction being given to the façade by the brilliant blending of the yellow bricks with red, so bright as to suggest the idea of their having been painted. A scrupulously clean stone at the front door, together with the bright green of the little palings and woodwork, told me what sort of landlady to expect, and I was not disappointed. A kindly featured woman, thin, cheery, and active, received us, speaking in that encouraging tone of half-compassionate, half-proprietary patronage, which I have observed so many women adopt towards lone beings of the opposite sex.

'You will find it precious dull, old man,' said Jones,

as we were eating our frugal dinner. 'There's nothing for you to do, unless you care to try a shot at the ducks over the mudflats. I shall be busy on and off nearly all tomorrow.'

As we talked, I could not help admiring the cheerful pluck with which Jones endured the terrible monotony of his life in this dreary place. His rector was said to be delicate, and in order to prolong a life, which no doubt he considered valuable to the Church, he lived with his family either at Torquay or Cannes in elegant idleness, quite unable to do any duty, but fully equal to enjoying the pleasant society of those charming places, and quite satisfied that he had done his duty when he sacrificed a tenth of his income to provide for the spiritual needs of his parish. There was no squire in the place; no 'gentle-folk', as the rustics called them, lived nearer than five miles; and there was not a single being of his own class with whom poor Jones could associate. And yet he made no complaint. The nearest approach to one being the remark that the worst of it was, it was so difficult, if not impossible, to be really understood. 'The poor being so suspicious and ignorant, they look at everything from such a low standpoint, enthusiasm and freshness sink so easily into formalism and listlessness.'

The next day, finding that I really could be of no use, and feeling awkward and bored, as a man always is when another is actively doing his duty, I went off to the marshes to see if I could get any sport.

I took some sandwiches and a flask with me, not intending to return until dinner. After wandering about for some time, crossing dyke after dyke by treacherous rails more or less rotten, I found myself on the edge of a wide mere. I could see some ducks out in the middle, and standing far out in the shallow water was a heron. They were all out of shot, and I saw I should do no good without a duckpunt.

I sat down on an old pile left on the top of the seawall, which had been lately repaired. The duck looked very tempting; but I doubted if I should do much good in broad daylight, even if I had a duck punt, without a duck gun. After sitting disconsolately for some time, I got up and wandered on.

The dreariness of the scene was most depressing: everything was brown and grey. Nothing broke the monotony of the wide-stretching mere; the whole scene gave me the impression of a straight line of interminable length, with a speck in the centre of it. That speck was myself.

At last, as I turned an angle in the seawall, I saw something lying above high-water mark, which looked like a boat.

Rejoiced to see any signs of humanity, I quickened my

pace. It was a boat, and, better still, a duck punt. As I came nearer I could see that she was old and very likely leaky; but here was a prospect of adventure, and I was not going to be readily daunted. On examination, the old craft seemed more watertight than I expected. At least she held water very well, and if she kept it in, she must equally well keep it out. I turned her over to run the water out, and then dragging the crazy old boat over the line of seaweed, launched her. But now a real difficulty met me. The paddles were nowhere to be seen. They had doubtless been taken away by the owner, and it would be little use searching for them. But a stout stick would do to punt her over the shallow water; and after some little search I found an old stake which would answer well.

This was real luck. I had now some hope of bagging a few ducks; at any rate, I was afloat, and could explore the little islets, which barely rose above the brown water. I might at least find some rabbits on them. I cautiously poled myself towards the black dots; but before I came within range, up rose first one, then another and another, like a string of beads, and the whole flight went, with outstretched necks and rapidly beating wings, away to my right, and seemed to pitch again beyond a low island some half-mile away. The heron had long ago taken himself off; so there was nothing to be done but pole across the mud in pursuit of the duck. I had not gone many yards when I found that I was going much faster than I expected, and soon saw the cause. The tide was falling, and I was being carried along with it. This would bring me nearer to my ducks, and I lazily guided the punt with the stake.

On rounding the island I found a new source of interest. The mere opened out to a much larger extent, and away towards my right I could see a break in the low land, as if a wide ditch had been cut through; while in this opening ever and anon dark objects rose up and disappeared again in a way I could not account for. The water seemed to be running off the mudflats, and I saw that if I did not wish to be left high, but not dry, on the long slimy wastes, I must be careful to keep in the little channels or 'lakes', which acted as natural drains to the acres of greasy mud.

A conspicuous object attracted my attention some mile or more towards the opening in the land. It was a vessel lying high up on the mud, and looking as if she was abandoned.

The ducks had pitched a hundred yards or so beyond the island, and I approached as cautiously as I could; but just as I was putting down the stake to take up my gun, there was a swift sound of beating wings and splashing water, and away my birds flew, low over the mud, towards the old hulk.

Here was a chance, I thought. If I could get on board and remain hidden, I might, by patiently waiting, get a shot. I looked at my watch; there was still plenty of daylight left, and the tide was only just beginning to leave the mud. I punted away, therefore, with renewed hope, and was not long in getting up to the old ship.

There was just sufficient water over the mud to allow me to approach within ten or twelve feet, but further I could not push the punt. This was disappointing; however, I noticed a deep lake ran round the other side, and determined to try my luck there. So with a slosh and a heave I got the flat afloat again, and made for the deeper water. It turned out quite successful, and I was enabled to get right under the square overhanging counter, while a little lane of water led alongside her starboard quarter. I pushed the nose of the punt into this, and was not long in clambering on board by the rusty irons of her forechains.

The old vessel lay nearly upright in the soft mud, and a glance soon told she would never be used again. Her gear and rigging were all rotten, and everything valuable had been removed. She was a brig of some two hundred tons, and had been a fine vessel, no doubt. To me there is always a world of romance in a deserted ship. The places she has been to, the scenes she has witnessed, the possibilities of crime, of adventure – all these thoughts crowd upon me when I see an old hulk lying deserted and forgotten – left to rot upon the mud of some lonely creek.

In order to keep my punt afloat as long as possible, I towed her round and moored her under the stern, and then looked over the bulwarks for the ducks. There they were, swimming not more than a hundred and fifty yards away, and they were coming towards me. I remained perfectly concealed under the high bulwark, and could see them paddling and feeding in the greasy weed. Their approach was slow, but I could afford to wait. Nearer and nearer they came; another minute, and they would be well within shot. I was already congratulating myself upon the success of my adventure, and thinking of the joy of Jones at this large accession to his larder, when suddenly there was a heavy splash, and with a wild spluttering rush the whole pack rose out of the water, and went skimming over the mud towards the distant sea. I let off both barrels after them, and tried to console myself by thinking that I saw the feathers fly from one; but not a bird dropped, and I was left alone in my chagrin.

What could have caused the splash, that luckless splash, I wondered. There was surely no one else on board the ship, and certainly no one could get out here without mudpattens or a boat. I looked round. All was perfectly still. Nothing broke the monotony of the grey scene – sodden and damp and lifeless. A chill breeze came up from the southwest, bringing with it a raw mist, which was blotting out the dark distance, and fast limiting my horizon. The day was drawing in, and I must be thinking of going home. As I turned round, my attention was arrested by seeing a duck punt glide past me in the now rapidly falling water, which was swirling by the mudbank on which the vessel lay. But there was no one in her. A dreadful thought struck me. It must be my boat, and how shall I get home? I ran to the stern and looked over. The duck punt was gone.

The frayed and stranded end of the painter told me how it had happened. I had not allowed for the fall of the tide, and the strain of the punt, as the water fell away, had snapped the line, old and rotten as it was.

I hurried to the bows, and jumping onto the bitts, saw my punt peacefully drifting away, some quarter of a mile off. It was perfectly evident I could not hope to get her again.

It was beginning to rain steadily. I could see that I was in for dirty weather, and became a little anxious about how I was to get back, especially as it was now rapidly growing dark. So thick was it that I could not see the low land anywhere, and could only judge of its position by remembering that the stern of the vessel pointed that way.

The conviction grew upon me that I could not possibly get away from this doleful old hulk without assistance, and how to get it, I could not for the life of me see. I had not seen a sign of a human being the whole day. It was not likely any more would be about at night. However, I shouted as loud as I could, and then waited to hear if there were any response. There was not a sound, only the wind moaned slightly through the stumps of the masts, and something creaked in the cabin.

Well, I thought, at least it might be worse. I shall have shelter for the night; while had I been left on one of these islands, I should have had to spend the night exposed to the pelting rain. Happy thought! Go below before it gets too dark, and see what sort of a berth can be got, if the worst comes to the worst. So thinking, I went to the booby hatch, and found as I expected that it was half broken open, and anyone could go below who liked.

As I stepped down the rotting companion, the air smelt foul and dank. I went below very cautiously, for I was not at all sure that the boards would bear me. It was fortunate I did so, for as I stepped off the lowest step the floor gave way under my foot, and had I not been holding on to the stair rail, I should have fallen through. Before going any further, I took a look round.

The prospect was not inviting. The light was dim; I

could scarcely make out objects near me, all else was obscurity. I could see that the whole of the inside of the vessel was completely gutted. What little light there was came through the stern ports. A small round speck of light looked at me out of the darkness ahead, and I could see that the flooring had either all given way or been taken out of her. At my feet a gleam of water showed me what to expect if I should slip through the floor joists.

Altogether, a more desolate, gloomy, ghostly place it would be difficult to find.

I could not see any bunk or locker where I could sit down, and everything movable had been taken out of the hulk. Groping my way with increasing caution, I stepped across the joists, and felt along the side of the cabin. I soon came to a bulkhead. Continuing to grope, I came to an opening. If the cabin was dim, here was blackness itself. I felt it would be useless to attempt to go further, especially as a very damp foul odour came up from the bilge water in her hold. As I stood looking into the darkness, a creepy, chilly shudder passed over me, and with a shiver I turned round to look at the cabin. My eyes had now become used to the gloom. A deeper patch of darkness on my right suggested the possibility of a berth, and groping my way over to it, I found the lower bunk was still entire. Here at least I could rest, if I found it impossible to get to shore. Having some wax vestas in my pocket, I struck a light and examined the bunk. It was better than I expected. If I could only find something to burn, I should be comparatively cheerful.

Before reconciling myself to my uncomfortable position, I resolved to see whether I could not get to the shore, and went up the rickety stairs again. It was raining hard, and the wind had got up. Nothing could be more dismal. I looked over the side and lowered myself down from the mainchains, to see if it were possible to walk over the mud. I found I could not reach the mud at all; and fearful of being unable to climb back if I let go, I clambered up the side again and got on board.

It was quite clear I must pass the night here. Before going below I once more shouted at the top of my voice, more to keep up my own spirits than with any hope of being heard, and then paused to listen. Not a sound of any sort replied. I now prepared to make myself as comfortable as I could.

It was a dreary prospect. I would rather have spent the night on deck than down below in that foul cabin; but the drenching driving rain, as well as the cold, drove me to seek shelter below. It seemed so absurd to be in the position of a shipwrecked sailor, within two or three miles of a prosy country hamlet, and in a landlocked harbour while actually on land, if the slimy deep mud could be called land. I had not many matches left, but I had my gun and cartridges. The idea occurred to me to fire off minute guns. 'That's what I ought to do, of course. The red flash will be seen in this dark night,' for it was dark now and no mistake. Getting up onto the highest part of the vessel, I blazed away. The noise sounded to me deafening; surely the whole countryside would be aroused. After firing off a dozen cartridges, I waited. But the silence only seemed the more oppressive, and the blackness all the darker. 'It's no good; I'll turn in,' I thought, dejectedly.

With great difficulty I groped my way to the top of the companion ladder, and bumped dismally down the steps. If only I had a light I should be fairly comfortable, I thought. 'Happy thought, make a "spit-devil!"' as we used, when boys, to call a little cone of damp gunpowder.

I got out my last two cartridges, and emptying the powder carefully into my hand, I moistened it, and worked it up to a paste. I then placed it on the smooth end of the rail, and lighted it. This was brilliant: at least so it seemed by contrast with the absolute blackness around me. By its light I was able to find my way to the bunk, and it lasted just long enough for me to arrange myself fairly comfortably for the night. By contriving a succession of matches, I was enabled to have enough light to see to eat my frugal supper; for I had kept a little sherry and a few sandwiches to meet emergencies, and it was a fortunate thing I had. The light and the food made me feel more cheery, and by the time the last match had gone out, I felt worse might have happened to me by a long way.

As I lay still, waiting for sleep to come, the absurdity of the situation forced itself upon me. Here was I, to all intents and purposes as much cut off from all communication with the rest of the world as if I were cast away upon a desert island. The chances were that I should make someone see or hear me the next day. Jones would be certain to have the country searched, and at the longest I should only endure the discomfort of one night, and get well laughed at for my pains; but meanwhile I was absolutely severed from all human contact, and was as isolated as Robinson Crusoe, only more so, for I had no other living thing whatever to share my solitude. The silence of the place was perfect; and if silence can woo sleep, sleep ought very soon to have come. But when one is hungry and wet, and in a strange uncanny kind of place, besides being in one's clothes, it is a very difficult thing to go to sleep. First, my head was too low; then, after resting it on my arms, I got cramp in them. My back seemed all over bumps; when I turned on my side, I appeared to have got a rather serious enlargement of the hip-joint; and I found my damp clothes smell very musty. After sighing and groaning for some time, I sat up for change of position, and nearly fractured my skull in so doing, against the remains of what had once been a berth above me. I didn't dare to move in the inky blackness, for I had seen sufficient to know that I might very easily break my leg or my neck in the floorless cabin.

There was nothing for it but to sit still, or lie down and wait for daylight. I had no means of telling the time. When I had last looked at my watch, before the last match had gone out, it was not more than six o'clock; it might be now about eight, or perhaps not so late. Fancy twelve long hours spent in that doleful black place, with nothing in the world to do to pass away the time! I must go to sleep; and so, full of this resolve, I lay down again.

I suppose I went to sleep. All I can recollect, after lying down, is keeping my mind resolutely turned inwards, as it were, and fixed upon the arduous business of counting an imaginary and interminable flock of sheep pass one by one through an ideal gate. This meritorious method of compelling sleep had, no doubt, been rewarded; but I have no means of knowing how long I slept, and I cannot tell at what hour of the night the following strange circumstances occurred – for occur they certainly did – and I am as perfectly convinced that I was the aural witness to some ghastly crime, as I am that I am writing these lines. I have little doubt I shall be laughed at, as Jones laughed at me – be told that I was dreaming, that I was overtired and nervous. In fact, so accustomed have I become to this sort of thing, that I now hardly ever tell my tale; or, if I do, I put it in the third person, and then I find people believe it, or at least take much more interest in it. I suppose the reason is, that people cannot bring themselves to think so strange a thing could have happened to such a prosy everyday sort of man as myself, and they cannot divest their minds of the idea that I am – well, to put it mildly – 'drawing on my imagination for facts.' Perhaps, if the tale appears in print, it will be believed, as a facetious friend of mine once said to a newly married couple, who had just seen the announcement of their marriage in *The Times*, 'Ah, didn't know you were married till you saw it in print!'

Well, be the time what it may have been, all I know is that the next thing I can remember after getting my five-hundredth sheep through the gate is, that I heard two most horrible yells ring through the darkness. I sat bolt-upright; and as a proof that my senses were 'all there,' I did not bring my head this time against the berth overhead, remembering to bend it outwards so as to clear it.

There was not another sound. The silence was as

absolute as the darkness. 'I must have been dreaming,' I thought; but the sounds were ringing in my ears, and my heart was beating with excitement. There must have been some reason for this. I never was 'taken this way' before. I could not make it out, and felt very uncomfortable. I sat there listening for some time. No other sound breaking the deathly stillness, and becoming tired of sitting, I lay down again. Once more I set myself to get my interminable flocks through that gate, but I could not help myself listening.

There seemed to me a sound growing in the darkness, a something gathering in the particles of the air, as if molecules of the atmosphere were rustling together, and with stilly movement were whispering something. The wind had died down, and I would have gone on deck if I could move; but it was hazardous enough moving about in the light: it would have been madness to attempt to move in that blackness. And so I lay still and tried to sleep.

But now there was a sound, indistinct, but no mere fancy; a muffled sound, as of some movement in the forepart of the ship.

I listened intently and gazed into the darkness.

What was the sound? It did not seem like rats. It was a dull, shuffling kind of noise, very indistinct, and conveying no clue whatever as to its cause. It lasted only for a short time. But now the cold damp air seemed to have become more piercingly chilly. The raw iciness seemed to strike into the very marrow of my bones, and my teeth chattered. At the same time a new sense seemed to be assailed: the foul odour which I had noticed arising from the stagnant water in the bilge appeared to rise into more objectionable prominence, as if it had been stirred.

'I cannot stand this,' I muttered, shivering in horrible aversion at the disgusting odour; 'I will go on deck at all hazards.'

Rising to put this resolve in execution, I was arrested by the noise beginning again. I listened. This time I distinctly distinguished two separate sounds: one, like a heavy soft weight being dragged along with difficulty; the other like the hard sound of boots on boards. Could there be others on board after all? If so, why had they made no sound when I clambered on deck, or afterwards, when I shouted and fired my gun?

Clearly, if there were people, they wished to remain concealed, and my presence was inconvenient to them. But how absolutely still and quiet they had kept! It appeared incredible that there should be anyone. I listened intently. The sound had ceased again, and once more the most absolute stillness reigned around. A gentle swishing, wobbling, lapping noise seemed to form itself in the darkness. It increased, until I recognised the chattering and bubbling of water. 'It must be the tide which is rising,' I thought; 'it has reached the rudder, and is eddying round the stern-post.' This also accounted, in my mind, for the other noises, because, as the tide surrounded the vessel, and she thus became waterborne, all kinds of sounds might be produced in the old hulk as she resumed her upright position.

However, I could not get rid of the chilly horrid feeling those two screams had produced, combined with the disgusting smell, which was getting more and more obtrusive. It was foul, horrible, revolting, like some carrion, putrid and noxious. I prepared to take my chances of damage, and rose up to grope my way to the companion-ladder.

It was a more difficult job than I had any idea of. I had my gun, it was true, and with it I could feel for the joists; but when once I let go of the edge of the bunk I had nothing to steady me, and nearly went headlong at the first step. Fortunately I reached back in time to prevent my fall; but this attempt convinced me that I had better endure the strange horrors of the unknown, than the certain miseries of a broken leg or neck.

I sat down, therefore, on the bunk.

Now that my own movements had ceased, I became

aware that the shuffling noise was going on all the time. 'Well,' thought I, 'they may shuffle. They won't hurt me, and I shall go to sleep again.' So reflecting, I lay down, holding my gun, ready to use as a club if necessary.

Now it is all very well to laugh at superstitious terrors. Nothing is easier than to obtain a cheap reputation for brilliancy, independence of thought, and courage, by deriding the fear of the supernatural when comfortably seated in a drawing room well lighted, and with company. But put those scoffers in a like situation with mine, and I don't believe they would have been any more free from a feeling the reverse of bold, mocking, and comfortable, than I was.

I had read that most powerful ghost story, 'The Haunted and the Haunters', by the late Lord Lytton, and the vividness of that weird tale had always impressed me greatly. Was I actually now to experience in my own person, and with no possibility of escape, the trying ordeal that bold ghosthunter went through, under much more favourable circumstances? He at least had his servant with him. He had fuel and a light, and above all, he could get away when he wanted to. I felt I could face any number of spiritual manifestations, if only I had warmth and light. But the icy coldness of the air was eating into my bones, and I shivered until my teeth chattered.

I could not get to sleep. I could not prevent myself

listening, and at last I gave up the contest, and let myself listen. But there seemed now nothing to listen to. All the time I had been refusing to let my ears do their office, by putting my handkerchief over one ear, and lying on my arm with the other, a confused noise appeared to reach me, but the moment I turned round and lay on my back, everything seemed quiet. 'It's only my fancy after all; the result of cold and want of a good dinner. I will go to sleep.' But in spite of this I lay still, listening a little longer. There was the sound of trickling water against the broad bilge of the old hulk, and I knew the tide was rising fast: my thoughts turned to the lost canoe, and to reproaching myself with my stupidity in not allowing enough rope, or looking at it more carefully. Suddenly I became all attention again. An entirely different sound now arrested me. It was distinctly a low groan, and followed almost immediately by heavy blows – blows which fell on a soft substance, and then more groans, and again those sickening blows.

'There must be men here. Where are they? And what is it?' I sat up, and strained my eyes towards where the sound came from. The sounds had ceased again. Should I call out, and let the man or men know that I was here? What puzzled me was the absolute darkness. How could anyone see to hit an object, or do anything else in this dense obscurity? It appalled me. Anything might pass at an inch's distance, and I could not tell who or what it was. But how could anything human find its way about, any more than I could? Perhaps there was a solid bulkhead dividing the forecastle from me. But it would have to be very sound, and with no chink whatever, to prevent a gleam or ray of light finding its way out somewhere. I could not help feeling convinced that the whole hull was open from one end to the other. Was I really dreaming after all? To convince myself that I was wide awake, I felt in my pockets for my notebook, and pulling out my pencil, I opened the book, and holding it in my left hand, wrote as well as I could, by feel alone: 'I am wide awake; it is about midnight – Christmas Eve, 187–.' I found I had got to the bottom of the page, so I shut the book up, resolving to look at it the next morning. I felt curious to see what the writing looked like by daylight.

But all further speculation was cut short by the shuffling and dragging noise beginning again. There was no doubt the sounds were louder, and were coming my way.

I never in all my life felt so uncomfortable – I may as well at once confess it – so frightened. There, in that empty hull, over that boardless floor, over these rotting joists, somebody or something was dragging some heavy weight. What, I could not imagine; only the shrieks, the blows, the groans, the dull thumping sounds, compelled me to suspect the worst – to feel convinced that I was actually within some few feet of a horrible murder then being committed. I could form no idea of who the victim was, or who was the assassin. That I actually heard the sounds I had no doubt; that they were growing louder and more distinct I felt painfully aware. The horror of the situation was intense. If only I could strike a light, and see what was passing close there – but I had no matches. I could hear a sound as of someone breathing slowly, stertorously, then a dull groan. And once more the cruel sodden blows fell again, followed by a drip, drip, and heavy drop in the dank water below, from which the sickening smell rose, pungent, reeking, horrible.

The dragging shuffling noise now began again. It came quite close to me, so close that I felt I had only to put out my hand to touch the thing. Good heavens! Was it coming to my bunk? The thing passed, and all the time the dull drip, as of some heavy drops, fell into the water below. It was awful. All this time I was sitting up, and holding my gun by its barrel, ready to use it if I were attacked. As the sound passed me at the closest, I put out the gun involuntarily, but it touched nothing, and I shuddered at the thought that there was no floor over which the weight could be drawn.

I must be dreaming some terribly vivid dream. It could not be real. I pinched myself. I felt I was pinching myself. It was no dream. The sweat poured off my brow, my teeth chattered with the cold. It was terrific in its dreadful mystery.

And now the sounds altered. The noises had reached the companion ladder. Something was climbing them with difficulty. The old stairs creaked. Bump, thump, the thing was dragged up the steps with many pauses, and at last it seemed to have reached the deck. A long pause now followed. The silence grew dense around. I dreaded the stillness – the silence that made itself be heard almost more than the sounds. What new horror would that awful quiet bring forth? What terror was still brooding in the depths of that clinging darkness – darkness that could be felt?

The absolute silence was broken – horribly broken – by a dull drip from the stairs, and then the dragging began again. Distant and less distinct, but the steps were louder. They came nearer – over my head – the old boards creaked, and the weight was dragged right over me. I could hear it above my head: for the steps stopped, and two distinct raps, followed by a third heavier one, sounded so clearly above me, that it seemed almost as if it was something striking the rotten wood-work of the berth over my head. The sounds were horribly suggestive of the elbows and head of a body being dropped on the deck.

And now, as if the horrors had not been enough, a fresh ghastliness was added. So close were the raps above me that I involuntarily moved, as if I had been struck by what caused them. As I did so, I felt something drop onto my head and slowly trickle over my forehead: it was too horrible! I sprang up in my disgust, and with a wild cry I stepped forward, and instantly fell between the joists into the rank water below.

The shock was acute. Had I been asleep and dreaming before, this must inevitably have roused me up. I found myself completely immersed in water, and, for a moment, was absolutely incapable of thinking. As it was pitch-dark and my head had gone under, I could not tell whether I was above water or not, as I felt the bottom and struggled and splashed onto my legs. It was only by degrees I knew I must be standing with my head out of the foul mixture, because I was able to breathe easily, although the wet running down from my hair dribbled into my mouth as I stood shivering and gasping.

It was astonishing how a physical discomfort overcame a mental terror. Nothing could be more miserable than my present position, and my efforts were at once directed to getting out of this dreadful place. But let anyone who has ever had the ill luck to fall out of bed in his boyhood try and recollect his sensations. The bewildering realisation that he is not in bed, that he does not know where he is, which way to go, or what to do to get back again; everything he touches seems strange, and one piece of furniture much the same as any other. I well remember such an accident, and how, having rolled under the bed before I was wide awake, I could not for the life of me understand why I could not get up, what it was that kept me down. I had not the least idea which way to get out, and kept going round and round in a circle under my bed for a long time, and should probably have been doing it until daylight, had not my sighs and groans awoke my brother, who slept in the same room, and who came to my help.

If, then, one is so utterly at fault in a room every inch of which one knows intimately, how much more hopeless was my position at the bottom of this old vessel, half immersed in water, and totally without any clue which could help me to get out! I had not the least idea which was the ship's stern or which her stem, and every movement I made with my feet only served to unsteady me, as the bottom was all covered with slime, and uneven with the great timbers of the vessel.

My first thought on recovering my wits was to stretch my arms up over my head, and I was relieved to find that I could easily reach the joists above me. I was always fairly good at gymnastics, and I had not much difficulty in drawing myself up and sitting on the joist, although the weight of my wet clothes added to my exertions considerably. Having so far succeeded, I sat and drained, as it were, into the water below. The smell was abominable. I never disliked myself so much, and I shivered with cold.

As I could not get any wetter, I determined to go on deck somehow, but where was the companion ladder? I had nothing to guide me. Strange to say, the reality of my struggles had almost made me forget the mysterious phenomena I had been listening to. But now, as I looked round, my attention was caught by a luminous patch which quivered and flickered on my right, at what distance from me I could not tell. It was like the light from a glow-worm, only larger and changing in shape; sometimes elongated like a lambent oval, and then it would sway one way or another, as if caught in a draught of air. While I was looking at it and wondering what could cause it, I heard the steps over my head; they passed above me, and then seemed to grow louder on my left. A creeping dread again came over me. If only I could get out of this horrible place – but where were the stairs? I listened. The footfall seemed to be coming down some steps; then the companion ladder must be on my left. But if I moved that way I should meet the Thing, whatever it was, that was coming down. I shuddered at the thought. However, I made up my mind. Stretching out my hand very carefully, I felt for the next joist, reached it, and crawled across. I stopped to listen. The steps were coming nearer. My hearing had now become acute; I could almost tell the exact place of each footfall. It came closer – closer – quite close, surely – on the very joist on which I was sitting. I thought I could feel the joist quiver, and involuntarily moved my hand to prevent the heavy tread falling on it. The steps passed on, grew fainter, and ceased, as they drew near the pale lambent light. One thing I noticed with curious horror, and that was, that although the thing must have passed between me and the light, yet it was never for a moment obscured, which it must have been had any body or substance passed between, and yet I was certain that the steps went directly from me to it.

It was all horribly mysterious; and what had become of the other sound – the thing that was being dragged? An irresistible shudder passed over me; but I determined to pursue my way until I came to something. It would never do to sit still and shiver there.

After many narrow escapes of falling again, I reached a bulkhead, and cautiously feeling along it, I came to an opening. It was the companion ladder. By this time my hands, by feeling over the joists, had become dry again. I felt along the step to be quite sure that it was the stairs, and in so doing I touched something wet, sticky, clammy.

Oh, horror! What was it? A cold shiver shook me nearly off the joist, and I felt an unutterable sense of repulsion to going on. However, the fresher air which came down the companion revived me, and, conquering my dread, I clambered onto the step. It did not take long to get upstairs and stand on the deck again.

I think I never in all my life experienced such a sense of joy as I did on being out of that disgusting hole. It was true I was soaking wet, and the night wind cut through me like a knife; but these were things I could understand, and were matter of common experience. What I had gone through might only be a question of nerves, and had no tangible or visible terror; but it was nonetheless very dreadful, and I would not go through such an experience again for worlds. As I stood cowering under the lee of the bulwark, I looked round at the sky. There was a pale light as if of daybreak away in the east, and it seemed as if all my troubles would be over with the dawn. It was bitterly cold. The wind had got round to the north, and I could faintly make out the low shore astern.

While I stood shivering there, a cry came down the wind. At first I thought it was a seabird, but it sounded again. I felt sure it was a human voice. I sprang up onto the taffrail, and shouted at the top of my lungs, then paused. The cry came down clearer and distinct. It was

Jones's voice – had he heard me? I waved my draggled pocket handkerchief and shouted again. In the silence which followed, I caught the words, 'We are coming.' What joyful words! Never did shipwrecked mariner on a lonely isle feel greater delight. My misery would soon be over. Anyhow, I should not have to wait long.

Unfortunately the tide was low, and was still falling. Nothing but a boat could reach me, I thought, and to get a boat would take some time. I therefore stamped up and down the deck to get warm; but I had an instinctive aversion for the companion ladder, and the deep shadows of the forepart of the vessel.

As I turned round in my walk, I thought I saw something moving over the mud. I stopped. It was undoubtedly a figure coming towards me. A voice hailed me in gruff accents –

'Lily, ahoy! Be anyone aboard?'

Was anyone aboard? What an absurd question! And here had I been shouting myself hoarse. However, I quickly reassured him, and then understood why my rescuer did not sink in the soft mud. He had mud pattens on. Coming up as close as he could, he shouted to me to keep clear, and then threw first one, then the other, clattering wooden board onto the deck. I found them, and under the instructions of my friend, I did not take long in putting them on. The man was giving me directions as to how to manage; but I did not care how much wetter I got, and dropped over the side into the slime. Sliding and straddling, I managed to get up to my friend, and then together we skated, as it were, to the shore – although skating very little represents the awkward splashes and slips I made on my way to land. I found quite a little crowd awaiting me on the bank; but Jones, with ready consideration, hurried me off to a cart he had in a lane near, and drove me home.

I told him the chief points of the adventure on our way but did not say anything of the curious noises. It is odd how shy a man feels at telling what he knows people will never believe. It was not until the evening of the next day that I began to tell him, and then only after I was fortified by an excellent dinner, and some very good claret. Jones listened attentively. He was far too kindly and well bred to laugh at me; but I could see he did not believe one word as to the reality of the occurrence. 'Very strange!' 'How remarkable!' 'Quite extraordinary!' he kept saying, with evident interest. But I was sure he put it all down to my fatigue and imagination. And so, to do him justice, has everybody else to whom I have told the tale since.

The fact is, we cannot, in this prosaic age, believe in anything the least approaching the supernatural. Nor do I. But nevertheless I am as certain as I am that I am writing these words, that the thing did really happen, and will happen again, may happen every night for all I know, only I don't intend to try and put my belief to the test. I have a theory which of course will be laughed at, and as I am not in the least scientific, I cannot bolster it up by scientific arguments. It is this: as Mr Edison has now discovered that by certain simple processes human sounds can be reproduced at any future date, so accidentally, and owing to the combination of most curious coincidences, it might happen that the agonised cries of some suffering being, or the sounds made by one at a time when all other emotions are as nothing compared to the supreme sensations of one committing some awful crime, could be impressed on the atmosphere or surface of an enclosed building, which could be reproduced by a current of air passing into that building under the same atmospheric conditions. This is the vague explanation I have given to myself.

However, be the explanation what it may, the facts are as I have stated them. Let those laugh who did not experience them. To return to the end of the story. There were two things I pointed out to Jones as conclusive that I was not dreaming. One was my pocketbook. I showed it him, and the words were quite clear – only, of course, very straggling. This is a facsimile of the writing, but I cannot account for the date being 1837 –

I am indeed
wake it is about
midnight Christmas
Eve 1837

The other point was the horrible stains on my hands and clothes. A foul-smelling dark chocolate stain was on my hair, hands, and clothes. Jones said, of course, this was from the rust off the mouldering ironwork, some of which no doubt had trickled down, owing to the heavy rain, through the defective caulking of the deck. The fact is, there is nothing that an ingenious mind cannot explain but the question is, Is the explanation the right one?

I could easily account for the phosphorescent light. The water was foul and stagnant, and it was no doubt caused by the same gases which produce the well-known ignis fatuus or Will-o'-the-wisp.

We visited the ship, and I recovered my gun. There were the same stains on the deck as there were on my clothes; and curiously enough they went in a nearly straight line over the place where I lay, from the top of the companion to the starboard bulwark. We carefully examined the forepart of the ship: it was as completely gutted as the rest of her. Jones was glad to get on deck again, as the atmosphere was very unpleasant, and I had no wish to stay.

At my request Jones made every inquiry he could about the old hulk. Not much was elicited. It bore an evil name, and no one would go on board who could help it. So far it looked as if it were credited with being haunted. The owner, who had been the captain of her, had died about three years before. His character did not seem amiable; but as he had left his money to the most influential farmer in the district, the country people were unwilling to talk against him.

I went with Jones to call on the farmer, and asked him point-blank if he had ever heard whether a murder had been committed on board the Lily. He stared at me, and then laughed. 'Not as I know of' was all his answer – and I never got any nearer than that.

I feel that this is all very unsatisfactory. I wish I could give some thrilling and sensational explanation. I am sorry I cannot. My imagination suggests many, as no doubt it will to each of my readers who possesses that faculty but I have only written this to tell the actual facts, not to add to our superabundant fiction.

If ever I come across any details bearing upon the subject, I will not fail to communicate them at once.

The vessel I found was the Lily of Goole, owned by one Master Gad Earwaker, and built in 1801.

The Step

E. F. BENSON

John Cresswell was returning home one night from the Britannia Club at Alexandria, where, as was his custom three or four times in the week, he had dined very solidly and fluidly, and played bridge afterwards as long as a table could be formed. It had been rather an expensive evening, for all his skill at cards had been unable to cope with such a continuous series of ill-favoured hands as had been his. But he had consoled himself with reasonable doses of whisky, and now he stepped homewards in very cheerful spirits, for his business affairs were going most prosperously and a loss of twenty-five or thirty pounds tonight would be amply compensated for in the morning. Besides, his bridge account for the year showed a credit which proved that cards were a very profitable pleasure.

It was a hot night of October, and, being a big plethoric man, he strolled at a very leisurely pace across the square and up the long street at the far end of which was his house. There were no taxis on the rank, or he would have taken one and saved himself this walk of nearly a mile; but he had no quarrel with that, for the night air with a breeze from the sea was refreshing after so long a session in a smoke-laden atmosphere. Above, a moon near to its full cast a very clear white light on his road. There was a narrow strip of sharp-cut shadow beneath the houses on his right, but the rest of the street and the pavement on the left of it, where he walked, were in bright illumination.

At first his way lay between rows of shops, European for the most part, with here and there a café where a few customers still lingered. Pleasant thoughts beguiled his progress; the Egyptian sugar crop, in which he was much interested, had turned out very well and he saw a big profit on his options. Not less satisfactory were other businesses in which he did not figure so openly. He lent money, for instance, on a large scale, to the native population, and these operations extended far up the Nile. Only last week he had been at Luxor, where he had concluded a transaction of a very remunerative sort. He had made a loan some months ago to a small merchant there and now the appropriate interest on this was in default: in consequence the harvest of a very fruitful acreage of sugarcane was his. A similar and even richer windfall had just come his way in Alexandria, for he had advanced money a year ago to a Levantine tobacco merchant on the security of his freehold store. This had brought him in very handsome interest, but a day or two ago the unfortunate fellow had failed, and Cresswell owned a most desirable freehold. The whole affair had been very creditable to his enterprise and sagacity, for he had privately heard that the municipality was intending to lay out the neighbourhood, a slum at present, where this store was situated, in houses of flats, and make it a residential quarter, and his newly acquired freehold would thus become a valuable property.

At present the tobacco merchant lived with his family in holes and corners of the store, and they must be evicted tomorrow morning. John Cresswell had already arranged for this, and had told the man that he would have to quit: he would go round there in the forenoon and see that they and their sticks of furniture were duly bundled out into the street. He would see personally that this was done, and looked forward to doing so. The old couple were beastly creatures, the woman a perfect witch who eyed him and muttered, but there was a daughter who was not ill-looking, and someone of the beggared family would be obliged to earn bread. He did not dwell on this, but the thought just flitted through his brain . . . Then doors would be locked and windows barred in the store that was now his, and he would lunch at the club afterwards. He was popular there; he had a jovial geniality about him, and a habit of offering drinks before they could be offered to him. That, too, was good for business.

Ten minutes' strolling brought him to the end of the shops and cafés that formed the street, and now the road ran between residential houses, each detached and with a space of garden surrounding it, where dry-leaved palms rattled in this wind from the sea. He was approaching the flamboyant Roman Catholic church, to which was attached a monastic establishment, a big white barrack-looking house where the Brothers of Poverty or some such order lived. Something to do with St. Mark, he vaguely remembered, who by tradition had brought Christianity to Egypt nearly nineteen hundred years ago. Often he met one of these odd sandal-footed creatures with his brown habit, his rosary and his cowled head going in or out of their gate, or toiling in their garden. He did not like them: lousy fellows he would have called them. Sometimes in their mendicant errands they came to his door asking alms for the indigent Copts. Not long ago he had found one actually ringing the bell of his front door, instead of going humbly round to the back, as befitted his quality, and Cresswell told him that he would loose his bulldog on the next of their breed who ventured within his garden gate. How the fellow had skipped off when he heard talk of the dog! He dropped one of his sandals in his haste to be gone, and not sparing the time to adjust it again, had hopped and hobbled over the sharp gravel to gain the street. Cresswell had laughed aloud to see his precipitancy, and the best of the joke was that he had not got any sort of dog on his premises at all. At the remembrance of that humorous incident he grinned to himself as he passed the porch of the church.

He paused a moment to mop his forehead and to light a cigarette, looking about him in great good humour. Before him and behind the road was quite empty: lights gleamed behind Venetian shutters from a few upper windows of the houses, but all the world was in bed or on its way there. There were still three or four hundred yards to go before he came to his house, and as he turned his face homewards again and walked a little more briskly, he heard a step behind him, sharp and distinct, not far in his rear. He paid no heed: someone, late like himself, was going home, walking in the same direction, for the step followed him.

His cigarette was ill-lit; a little core of burning stuff fell from it onto the pavement and he stopped to rekindle it. Possibly some subconscious region of his mind was occupied with the step which had sprung up so oddly behind him in the empty street, for while he was getting his cigarette to burn again he noticed that the step had ceased. It was hardly worthwhile to turn round (so little the matter interested him), but a casual glance showed him that the wayfarer must have turned into one of the houses he had just passed, for the whole street, brightly moonlit, was as empty as when he surveyed it a few minutes before. Soon he came to his own gate and clanged it behind him.

The eviction of the Levantine merchant took place in the morning, and Cresswell watched his porters carrying out the tawdry furniture – a few tables, a few chairs, a sofa covered in tattered crimson plush, a couple of iron bedsteads, a bundle of dirty sheets and blankets. He was not certain in his own mind whether these paltry articles did not by rights belong to him, but they were fit for nothing except the dust heap, and he had no use for them. There they stood in the clean bright sunshine, rubbish and no more, blocking the pavement, and a policeman told their owner that he had best clear them away at once unless he wanted trouble. There was the usual scene to which he was quite accustomed: the man's wife snivelling and slovenly, witchlike and early old, knelt and kissed his hand, and wheezingly besought his compassion. She called him 'Excellency', she promised him her prayers, which he desired as little as her pots and pans. She invoked blessings on his head, for she knew that out of his pity he would give them a little more time. They had nowhere to go nor any roof to shelter them: her husband had money owing to him, and he would collect these debts and pay his default as sure as there was a God in heaven. This was a changed note from her mutterings of yesterday, but of course Cresswell had a deaf ear for this oily rigmarole, and presently he went into the store to see that everything had been removed.

It was in a filthy, dirty state; floors were rotten and the paint peeling, but the whole place would soon be broken up and he was not going to spend a piastre on it, so long as the ground on which it stood was his. Then he saw to the barring of the windows and the doors, and he gave the policeman quite a handsome tip to keep an eye on the place and take care that these folk did not get ingress again. When he came out, he found that the old man had procured a handcart, and he and his son were loading it up, so of course they had somewhere to go: it was all a pack of lies about their being homeless. The old hag was squatting against the house wall, but now there were no more prayers and blessings for him, and she had taken to her mutterings again. As for the daughter, seen in the broad daylight, she had a handsome face, but she was sullen and dirty and forbidding, and he gave no further thought to her. He hailed a taxi and went off to the club for lunch.

Though Cresswell, in common parlance, 'did himself well', taking his fill of food and drink and tobacco, he was also careful of that great strong body of his, and the occasions were few when he omitted, at the end of the day's work, to walk out in the direction of Ramleh for a brisk hour or two, or, during the hotter months, to have a good swim in the sea and a bask in the sun. On the day following this eviction he took a tramp along the firm sands of the coast, and then, turning inland, struck the road that would bring him back to his own house. This stood quite at the end of the rows of detached houses past which he had walked two evenings before: beyond, the road ran between tumbled sand dunes and scrub-covered flats. Here and there in sheltered hollows a few Arab goatherds and such had made themselves nomadic tentlike habitations of a primitive sort: half a dozen posts set in the sand supported a roof of rugs and blankets stitched together. If they encroached too near the outskirts of the town the authorities periodically made a clearance of them, for they were apt to be light-fingered, pilfering folk, whose close vicinity was not desirable.

Today as he returned from his walk, Cresswell saw that a tent of this kind had newly been set up within twenty yards of his own garden wall. That would not do at all, that must be seen to, and he determined as soon as he had had his bath and his change of clothes to ring up his very good friend the chief inspector of police and request its removal. As he got nearer to it he saw that it was not quite of the usual type. The roof was clearly an outworn European carpet, and standing outside it on the sand were chairs and a sofa. Somehow these seemed familiar to him, though he could not localize the association. Then out of the tent came that old Levantine hag who had kissed his hand and knelt to him yesterday, invoking on him all sorts of blessings and prosperities, if only he would have compassion. She saw him, for now not more than a few dozen yards separated them, and then, suddenly pointing at him, she broke out into a gabble and yell of curses. That made him smile.

'So you've changed your tune again, have you?' he thought, 'for that doesn't sound much like good wishes. Curse away, old woman, if it relieves your mind, for it doesn't hurt me. But you'll have to be shifting once more, for I'm not going to have you and your like squatting there.'

Cresswell rang up his friend the chief inspector of police, and was most politely told that matter should be seen to in the morning. Sure enough when he set out to go to his office next day, he saw that it was being attended to, for the European carpet which had served for a roof was already down, and the handcart was being laden with the stuff. He noticed, quite casually, that the two women and the boy were employed in lading it; the Levantine was lying on the sand and taking no part in the work. Two days later he had occasion to pass the pauper cemetery of Alexandria, where the poorest kind of funeral was going on. The coffin was being pushed to the side of the shallow grave on a handcart: a boy and two women followed it. He could see who they were.

He dined that night at the club in rare good humour with the affairs of life. Already the municipality had offered him for his newly acquired freehold a sum that was double the debt for which it had been security, and though possibly he might get more if he stuck out for a higher price he had accepted it, and the money had been paid into his bank that day. To get a hundred per cent in a week was very satisfactory business, and who knew but that some new scheme of improvement might cause them to change their plans, leaving him with a ramshackle building on his hands for which he had no manner of use? He enjoyed his dinner and his wine, and particularly did he enjoy the rubber of bridge that followed. All went well with his finesses; he doubled his adversaries two or three times with the happiest results, they doubled him and were sorry for having spoken, and there would be a very pleasant item to enter in his card account that evening.

It was later than usual when he quitted the club. Just outside there was a beggar woman squatting at the edge of the pavement, who held her palm towards him and whined out blessings. Good-naturedly he fumbled in his pocket for a couple of piastres, and the blessings poured out in greater shrillness and copiousness as she pushed back the black veil that half shrouded her face to thank him for his beneficence to the needy widow. Next moment she threw his alms on the pavement, she spat at him, and like a moth she flitted away into the shadows.

Cresswell recognized her even as she had recognized him and picked up his piastres. It was amusing to think that the old hag so hated him that even his alms were abhorrent to her. 'I'll drop them into that collecting box outside the church,' he thought to himself.

Tonight, late though it was, there were many folk about in the square, natives for the most part, padding softly along, and there were still a few taxis on the rank. But he preferred to walk home, for he had been so busy all day that he had given his firm fat body no sort of exercise. So crossing the square he went up the street which led to his house. Here the cafés were already closed, and soon the pavements grew empty. The waning moon had risen, and though the lights of the street grew more sparse as he emerged into the residential quarter, his way lay bright before him. In his hand he still held the two piastres which had been flung back at him ready for the collection box. He walked briskly, for the night was cool, and it was no exercise to saunter. Not a breath of wind stirred the air, and the clatter of the dry palm leaves was dumb.

He was now approaching the Roman Catholic church, when a step suddenly sounded out crisp and distinct behind him. He remembered then for the first time what had happened some nights ago and halted and listened: not a sound broke the stillness. He whisked round, but the street seemed empty. On he went again, now more slowly, and there was the following step again, neither gaining on him nor falling behind; to judge by the loudness of it, it could not be more than a dozen paces in his rear. Then a very obvious explanation occurred to him: no doubt this was some echo of his own footsteps. He went more quickly, and the steps behind him quickened; he stopped and they stopped. The whole thing was clear enough, and not a shadow of uneasiness, or anything approaching it, was in his mind. He slipped his ironical alms into the collecting box outside the church, and was amused to hear that they evoked no tinkle from within. 'Quite a little windfall for those brown-gowned fellows; they'll buy another rosary,' he said to himself, and soon, with the echo of his own steps following, he turned in at his gate. Once inside, he slipped behind a myrtle bush that stood at the edge of the gravel walk, to see if by chance anyone passed on the road outside. But nothing happened, and his theory of the echo, though it was odd that he should never have noticed it till so lately, seemed quite confirmed.

From that night onwards he made it a practice, if he dined at the club, to walk home. Sometimes the step followed him, but not always, and this was an objection to that sensible echo theory. But the matter was no sort of worry to him except sometimes when he woke in the night, and found that his brain, still drowsy and not in complete control, was brooding over it with an ever-increasing preoccupation. Often that misgiving faded away and he dropped off to dreamless sleep again; some-times it was sufficiently disquieting to bring him broad awake, and then with all his senses about him, it vanished. But there was this condition, halfway between waking and sleeping, when in the twilight chamber of his brain something listened, something feared. When fully awake he no more thought of it than he thought of that frowsy Levantine tobacco merchant whom he had evicted and whose funeral he chanced to have seen.

Early in December his cousin and partner in the sugar business came down from Cairo to spend a week with him. Bill Cresswell may be succinctly described as 'a hot lot', and often after dinner at the club he left his cousin to his cronies and the sedater pleasures of bridge, and went out with a duplicate latchkey in his pocket on livelier private affairs. One night, the last of Bill's sojourn here, there was 'nothing doing' and the two set forth together homewards from the club.

'Nice night, let's walk,' said John. 'Nothing like a walk when there's liquid on board. Clears the brain for you and I must have a final powwow tonight, if you're off tomorrow. There are some bits of things still to go through.'

Bill acquiesced. The cafés were all closed, there was nothing very promising.

'Night life here ain't a patch on Cairo,' he observed. 'Everyone seems to go to bed here just about when we begin to get going. Not but what I haven't enjoyed my stay with you. Capital good fellows at your club and brandy to match.'

He stopped and ruefully scanned the quiet and emptiness of the street.

'Not a soul anywhere,' he said. 'Shutters up, all gone to bed. Nothing for it but a powwow, I guess.'

They walked on in silence for a while. Then behind them, firm and distinct to John's ears, there sprang up the sound of the footsteps, for which now he knew that he waited and listened. He wheeled round.

'What's up?' asked Bill.

'Curious thing,' said John. 'Night after night now, though not every night, when I walk home, I hear a step following me. I heard it then.'

Bill gave a vinous giggle.

'No such luck for me,' he said. 'I like to hear a step following me about one of a morning. Something agreeable may come of it. Wish I could hear it.'

They walked on, and again, clearer than before, John heard what was inaudible to the other. He told himself, as he often did now, that it was an echo. But it was odd that the echo only repeated the footfalls of one of them. As he recognized this, he felt for the first time, when he was fully awake, some sudden chill of fear. It was as if a cold hand closed for a moment on his heart, just pressing it softly, almost tenderly. But they were now close to his own gate, and presently it clanged behind them.

Bill returned next day to the gladder life of Cairo. John Cresswell saw him off at the station and was passing out into the street again through the crowd of loungers and porters and passengers when there defined itself to his ear the sound of that footstep which he now knew so well. How he recognized it and isolated it from the tread of so many other feet he had no idea: simply his brain told him that it was following him again. He took a taxi to his office, and as he mounted the white stone stairs once more it was on his track. Once more the gentle pressure of cold fingers seemed to assure him of the presence that, though invisible, was very close to him, and now it was as if those fingers were pressed on some bell push in his brain, and there sounded out a shrill tingle of fear. So hard-headed and sensible a man, of course, had nothing but scorn for all the claptrap bogy tales of spirits and ghosts and hauntings, and he would have welcomed any sort of apparition in which the step manifested itself, in order to have the pleasure of laughing in its face. He would have liked to see a skeleton or some shrouded figure stand close to him; he would have slashed at it with his stick and convinced himself that there was nothing there. Whatever his own eyes appeared to see could not be so unnerving as these tokens of the invisible.

A stiff drink pulled him together again, and for the rest of the day there occurred no repetition of that tapping step which had begun to sprout with terror for him. In any case he was determined to fight it, for he realized that it was chiefly his own fear that troubled him. No doubt he was suffering from some small nervous derangement; he had been working very hard, and after Christmas, if the thing continued to worry him, probably he would see a doctor, who would prescribe him some tonic or some sedative which would send the step into the limbo from which it had come. But it was more probable that his cure was in his own hands: his own resistance was all the medicine he needed.

It was in pursuance of this very sane policy that he set out that night after an evening at the club to walk home: he faced it just because he knew that some black well was digging itself into his soul. To yield, to take a taxi, was to retreat, and if he did that, if he gave way an inch, he guessed that he might be soon flying in panic before an invading and imaginary host of phantoms. He had no use for phantoms; the solid satisfactions of life were enough occupation. Once more, as he drew near the church, the step sprang up, and now he sought no longer to tell himself it was an echo. Instead he fixed his mind on it, saying to himself, 'There it is and it can't hurt me. Let it walk all day and night behind me if it chooses. It's got a fancy for me.' Then his garden gate shut behind him, and with a sigh of relief he knew that he had passed out of its beat, for when once he was within, it never came farther.

He stood for a moment on his threshold, after he had opened his door, pleased with himself for having faced it. The bright light shone full onto the straight gravel walk he had just traversed. It was quite empty, and nothing was looking in through his gate. Then he heard from close at hand the crunch of the gravel underneath the heel of some invisible wayfarer. Now was the time to assert himself again, to look his fear in the eyes and mock at it.

'Come along, whoever you are,' he called, 'and have a drink before you get back to hell. Something cooling. Drop of cold water, isn't it?'

Thick sweat had broken out on his forehead, and his hand on the door knob shook as with ague as he stood there looking out onto the bright empty path. But he did not flinch from the lesson he was teaching himself. The seconds ticked away: he could count them from the pulse that hammered in his throat. 'I'll give it a hundred beats,' he said to himself, 'and then I'll say goodnight to Mr. Nothing-at-all.'

He counted his hundred, he gave ten beats more for good luck. 'Goodnight, you old fraud,' he said, and went in and secured the door.

It seemed indeed for the week that followed that he had rightly gauged the nature of the hallucination which had threatened to establish its awful dominion over him. Never once, whether by day or night, did there come to his ears that footfall which he feared and listened for, nor, if in the dead hours of the darkness he lay for a while between sleep and waking, did he quake with a sense that something unseen and aware was watching him. A little courage, a flat denial of his fears had been sufficient not only to scotch them, but to snuff out the manifestation which had caused them. He kept his thoughts well in hand, he would not even conjecture what had been the cause of that visitation. Occasionally, while it still vexed him, he had cast about for the origin of it, he had wondered whether that shrill Levantine hag calling curses on him could somehow have found root in his mind. But now it was past and done with: he would have a few days' remission from work, if it was overwork that had been at the bottom of it, at Christmas, and perhaps it would be prudent not to be quite so free with the club brandy.

On Christmas Eve he and his friends sat at their bridge till close on midnight, then lingered over a drink, wished each other seasonable greetings and dispersed. Cresswell hesitated as to whether he should not take a taxi home, for the object with which he had trudged back there so often seemed to be gained, and he no longer feared the recurrence of the step. But he thought he would just set the seal on his victory and went on foot.

He had come to the point in his walk where he had first heard the step. Tonight, as usual, there was none, and he stopped a moment looking round him securely and serenely. It was a bright night, luminous with a moon a little after the full, and it amazed him to think that he had ever fashioned a terror to himself in this quiet, orderly street. From not far ahead there came the sound of the bells of the church saluting Christmas morning. They would have been holding their midnight Mass there. He breathed the night air with content, and throwing the butt of his spent cigar into the roadway, he walked on again.

With a sudden sinking of his heart, he heard behind him the step which he thought he had silenced forever. It was faint at first, but tonight, instead of keeping at a uniform distance behind him, it was approaching. Louder and more crisp it sounded, until it was close to him. On and on it came, still gaining on him, and now there brushed by him, though not quite touching him, the figure of a man in European dress, with his head wrapped in a shawl.

'Hullo, you there,' called Cresswell. 'You're the skunk who's been following me, are you, and slipping out of sight again? No more of your damned conjuring tricks. Let's have a look at you.'

The figure, now some two or three yards ahead of him, stopped at the sound of his voice and turned round. The shawl covered its face, but for a narrow chink between the edges.

'So you understand English,' said Cresswell. 'Now I'll thank you to take that shawl off your face, and let me see who it is that's been dogging me.'

The man raised his hands and threw back the shawl.

The moonlight shone on his face, and that face was just a slab of smooth yellowish flesh extending from ear to ear, empty as the oval of an egg without eyes or nose or mouth. From the upper edge of the shawl where it crossed the forehead there depended a few wisps of grey hair.

Cresswell looked, and a wave of panic fear submerged his very soul. He gave a little thin squeal and started to run, listening the while in an agony of terror to hear if the steps of that nameless, faceless, creature were following. He must run, he must run, to get away from that thing out of hell which had manifested itself.

Then close at hand he saw the lights of the church, and there perhaps he could find sanctuary from it. The door was open, and he sprang up the steps. Close by there were lights burning on the altar of a side chapel, and he flung himself on his knees. Not for years had he attempted to pray, and now in the agony of his soul he could but say in a gabbling whisper, 'O my God: O my God.' Over and over he said it.

By degrees some sort of self-control came back to him. There were holy images, there was a sacred picture above the altar, a smell of hallowing incense was in the air. Surely there was protection here, a power that would intervene between him and the terror of that face. A sort of tranquility overscored his panic, and he began to look round.

The church was darker than it had been when he entered, and he saw that some of those cowled brown-habited men of the order were moving quietly about, quenching the lights. Those at the altar in front of which he knelt were still bright, and now he saw one of these cowled figures move up close to him, as if waiting for him to finish his devotions. He was calm now, his panic had quite passed, and he rose from his knees.

'I've had a terrible fright, Father,' he said to the monk. 'I saw something just now out in the street which must have come out of hell.'

The figure turned a little towards him: the cowl concealed its face altogether, and the voice came muffled.

'Indeed, my son,' he said. 'Tell me what it is that frightened you.'

Cresswell felt some backwash of his panic returning.

'A man passed me as I was going back to my house,' he said, 'and I told him to stop and let me have a look at him. He wore a shawl over his head and he threw it back. Oh, my God, that face!'

The monk quietly raised his hands and grasped the edges of his cowl. Then with a quick movement he threw it back.

'That sort of face?' he said.

The Vanishing House

BERNARD CAPES

'My grandfather,' said the banjo, 'drank "dog's-nose,"
my father drank "dog's-nose," and I drink "dog's-nose."
If that ain't heredity, there's no virtue in the board
schools.'

'Ah!' said the piccolo, 'you're always a-boasting of your
science. And so, I suppose, your son'll drink "dog's-nose,"
too?'

'No,' retorted the banjo, with a rumbling laugh, like
wind in the bunghole of an empty cask; 'for I ain't got
none. The family ends with me; which is a pity, for I'm
a full stop to be proud on.'

He was an enormous, tun-bellied person – a mere
mound of expressionless flesh, whose size alone was an
investment that paid a perpetual dividend of laughter.
When, as with the rest of his company, his face was

159

blackened, it looked like a specimen coal on a pedestal in a museum.

There was Christmas company in the Good Intent, and the sanded taproom, with its trestle tables and sprigs of holly stuck under sooty beams reeked with smoke and the steam of hot gin and water.

'How much could you put down of a night, Jack?' said a little grinning man by the door.

'Why,' said the banjo, 'enough to lay the dustiest ghost as ever walked.'

'*Could* you, now?' said the little man.

'Ah!' said the banjo, chuckling. 'There's nothing like settin' one spent to lay another; and there I could give you proof number two of heredity.'

'What! Don't you go for to say you ever see'd a ghost!'

'Haven't I? What are you whisperin' about, you blushful chap there by the winder?'

'I was only remarkin', sir, 'twere snawin' like the devil.'

'*Is* it? Then the devil has been misjudged these eighteen hundred and ninety odd years.'

'But *did* you ever see a ghost?' said the little grinning man, pursuing his subject.

'No, I didn't, sir,' mimicked the banjo, 'saving in coffee grounds. But my grandfather in *his* cups see'd one; which brings us to number three in the matter of heredity.'

'Give us the story, Jack,' said the 'bones,' whose agued shins were extemporizing a rattle on their own account before the fire.

'Well, I don't mind,' said the fat man. 'It's seasonable; and I'm seasonable, like the blessed plum pudden, I am; and the more burnt brandy you set about me, the richer and headier I'll go down.'

'You'd be a jolly old pudden to digest,' said the piccolo.

'You blow your aggrawation into your pipe and sealing-wax the stops,' said his friend.

He drew critically at his 'churchwarden' a moment or so, leaned forward, emptied his glass into his capacious receptacles, and, giving his stomach a shift, as if to accommodate it to its new burden, proceeded as follows:

'Music and malt is my nat'ral inheritance. My grandfather blew his "dog's-nose," and drank his clarinet like a artist; and my father—'

'What did you say your grandfather did?' asked the piccolo.

'He played the clarinet.'

'You said he blew his "dog's-nose."'

'Don't be a ass, Fred!' said the banjo, aggrieved. 'How the blazes could a man blow his dog's nose, unless he muzzled it with a handkercher, and then twisted its tail? He played the clarinet, I say; and my father played the musical glasses, which was a form of harmony pertiklerly genial to him. Amongst us we've piped out a good long century – ah! we have, for all I look sich a babby bursting on sops and spoon meat.'

'What!' said the little man by the door. 'You don't include them cockt hatses in your expeerunce?'

'My grandfather wore 'em, sir. He wore a play-actin' coat, too, and buckles to his shoes, when he'd got any; and he and a friend or two made a permanency of "waits" (only they called 'em according to the season), and got their profit goin' from house to house, principally in the country, and discoursin' music at the low rate of whatever they could get for it.'

'Ain't you comin' to the ghost, Jack?' said the little man hungrily.

'All in course, sir. Well, gentlemen, it was hard times pretty often with my grandfather and his friends, as you may suppose; and never so much as when they had to trudge it across country, with the nor'-easter buzzin' in their teeth and the snow piled on their cockt hats like lemon sponge on entry dishes. The rewards, I've heard him say – for he lived to be ninety, nevertheless – was poor compensation for the drifts, and the influenza, and the broken chilblains; but now and again they'd get a fair skinful of liquor from a jolly squire, as 'd set 'em up like boggarts mended wi' new broomsticks.'

'Ho-haw!' broke in a hurdle-maker in a corner; and

then, regretting the publicity of his merriment, put his fingers bashfully to his stubble lips.

'Now,' said the banjo, 'it's of a pertikler night and a pertikler skinful that I'm a-going to tell you; and that night fell dark, and that skinful were took a hundred years ago this December, as I'm a Jack pudden!'

He paused a moment for effect, before he went on:

'They were down in the sou'-west country, which they little knew; and were anighing Winchester city, or should 'a' been. But they got muzzed on the ungodly downs, and before they guessed, they was off the track. My good hat! there they was, as lost in the snow as three nutshells a-sinkin' into a hasty pudden. Well, they wandered round; pretty confident at first, but getting madder and madder as every sense of their bearings slipped from them. And the bitter cold took their vitals, so as they saw nothing but a great winding sheet stretched abroad for to wrap their dead carcasses in.

'At last my grandfather he stopt and pulled hisself together with an awful face, and says he:

"We're Christmas pie for the carrying-on crows if we don't prove ourselves human. Let's fetch out our pipes and blow our trouble into 'em." So they stood together, like as if they was before a house and they played "Kate of Aberdare" mighty dismal and flat, for their fingers froze to the keys.

'Now, I tell you, they hadn't climbed over the first stave, when there come a skin of wind and spindrift of snow as almost took them off of their feet; and, on the going down of it, Jem Sloke, as played the hautboy, dropped the reed from his mouth, and called out, "Sakes alive! If we fools ain't been standin' outside a gentleman's gate all the time, and not knowin' it!"

'You might 'a' knocked the three of 'em down wi' a barley straw, as they stared and stared, and then fell into a low, enjoyin' laugh. For they was standin' not six fut from a tall iron gate in a stone wall, and behind these was a great house showin' out dim, with the winders all lighted up.

'"Lord!" chuckled my grandfather, "to think o' the tricks o' this vaganious country! But, as we're here, we'll go on and give 'em a taste of our quality."

'They put new heart into the next movement, as you may guess; and they hadn't fair started on it, when the door of the house swung open, and down the shaft of light that shot out as far as the gate there come a smiling young gal, with a tray of glasses in her hands.

'Now she come to the bars, and she took and put a glass through, not sayin' nothin', but invitin' someone to drink with a silent laugh.

'Did anyone take that glass? Of course he did, you'll be thinkin', and you'll be thinkin' wrong. Not a man of the three moved. They was struck like as stone, and their lips was gone the colour of sloe berries. Not a man took the glass. For why? The moment the gal presented it, each saw the face of a thing lookin' out of the winder over the porch, and the face was hidjus beyond words, and the shadder of it, with the light behind, stretched out and reached to the gal, and made her hidjus, too.

'At last my grandfather give a groan and put out his hand; and, as he did it, the face went, and the gal was beautiful to see agen.

'"Death and the devil!" said he. "It's one or both, either way; and I prefer 'em hot to cold!"

'He drank off half the glass, smacked his lips, and stood staring a moment.

'"Dear, dear!" said the gal, in a voice like falling water, "you've drunk blood, sir!"

'My grandfather gave a yell, slapped the rest of the liquor in the faces of his friends, and threw the cup agen the bars. It broke with a noise like thunder, and at that he up'd with his hands and fell full length into the snow.'

There was a pause. The little man by the door was twisting nervously in his chair.

'He came to – of course, he came to?' said he at length.

'He come to,' said the banjo solemnly, 'in the bitter break of dawn; that is, he come to as much of hisself as he ever was after. He give a squiggle and lifted his head;

and there was he and his friends a-lyin' on the snow of the high downs.'

'And the house and the gal?'

'Narry a sign of either, sir, but just the sky and the white stretch, and one other thing.'

'And what was that?'

'A stain of red sunk in where the cup had spilt.' There was a second pause, and the banjo blew into the bowl of his pipe.

'They cleared out of that neighbourhood double quick, you'll bet,' said he. 'But my grandfather was never the same man agen. His face took purple, while his friends' only remained splashed with red, same as birth marks; and, I tell you, if he ever ventur'd upon "Kate of Aberdare", his cheeks swelled up to the reed of his clarinet, like as a blue plum on a stalk. And forty year after, he died of what they call solution of blood to the brain.'

'And you can't have better proof than that,' said the little man.

'That's what *I* say,' said the banjo. 'Next player, gentlemen, please.'

Someone in the Lift

L. P. HARTLEY

'There's someone coming down in the lift, Mummy!'

'No, my darling, you're wrong, there isn't.'

'But I can see him through the bars – a tall gentleman.'

'You think you can, but it's only a shadow. Now, you'll see, the lift's empty.'

And it always was.

This piece of dialogue, or variations of it, had been repeated at intervals ever since Mr and Mrs Maldon and their son Peter had arrived at the Brompton Court Hotel, where, owing to a domestic crisis, they were going to spend Christmas. New to hotel life, the little boy had never seen a lift before and he was fascinated by it. When either of his parents pressed the button to summon it he would take up his stand some distance away to watch it coming down.

The ground floor had a high ceiling so the lift was visible for some seconds before it touched floor level: and it was then, at its first appearance, that Peter saw the figure. It was always in the same place, facing him in the left-hand corner. He couldn't see it plainly, of course, because of the double grille, the gate of the lift and the gate of the lift shaft, both of which had to be firmly closed before the lift would work.

He had been told not to use the lift by himself – an unnecessary warning, because he connected the lift with the things that grown-up people did, and unlike most small boys he wasn't over-anxious to share the privileges of his elders: he was content to wonder and admire. The lift appealed to him more as magic than as mechanism. Acceptance of magic made it possible for him to believe that the lift had an occupant when he first saw it, in spite of the demonstrable fact that when it came to rest, giving its fascinating click of finality, the occupant had disappeared.

'If you don't believe me, ask Daddy,' his mother said.

Peter didn't want to do this, and for two reasons, one of which was easier to explain than the other.

'Daddy would say I was being silly,' he said.

'Oh no, he wouldn't, he never says you're silly.'

This was not quite true. Like all well-regulated modern fathers, Mr Maldon was aware of the danger of offending a son of tender years: the psychological results might be regrettable. But Freud or no Freud, fathers are still fathers, and sometimes when Peter irritated him Mr Maldon would let fly. Although he was fond of him, Peter's private vision of his father was of someone more authoritative and awe-inspiring than a stranger, seeing them together, would have guessed.

The other reason, which Peter didn't divulge, was more fantastic. He hadn't asked his father because, when his father was with him, he couldn't see the figure in the lift.

Mrs Maldon remembered the conversation and told her husband of it. 'The lift's in a dark place,' she said, 'and I dare say he does see something, he's so much nearer to the ground than we are. The bars may cast a shadow and make a sort of pattern that we can't see. I don't know if it's frightening him, but you might have a word with him about it.'

At first Peter was more interested than frightened. Then he began to evolve a theory. If the figure only appeared in his father's absence, didn't it follow that the figure might be, could be, must be, his own father? In what region of his consciousness Peter believed this it would be hard to say; but for imaginative purposes he did believe it and the figure became for him 'Daddy in the lift'. The thought of Daddy in the lift did frighten him, and the neighbourhood of the lift shaft, in which he felt compelled to hang about, became a place of dread.

Christmas Day was drawing near and the hotel began to deck itself with evergreens. Suspended at the foot of the staircase, in front of the lift, was a bunch of mistletoe, and it was this that gave Mr Maldon his idea.

As they were standing under it, waiting for the lift, he said to Peter:

'Your mother tells me you've seen someone in the lift who isn't there.'

His voice sounded more accusing than he meant it to, and Peter shrank.

'Oh, not now,' he said, truthfully enough. 'Only sometimes.'

'Your mother told me that you always saw it,' his father said, again more sternly than he meant to. 'And do you know who I think it may be?'

Caught by a gust of terror Peter cried, 'Oh, please don't tell me!'

'Why, you silly boy,' said his father reasonably. 'Don't you want to know?'

Ashamed of his cowardice, Peter said he did.

'Why, it's Father Christmas, of course!'

Relief surged through Peter.

'But doesn't Father Christmas come down the chimney?' he asked.

'That was in the old days. He doesn't now. Now he takes the lift!'

Peter thought a moment.

'Will you dress up as Father Christmas this year,' he asked, 'even though it's an hotel?'

'I might.'

'And come down in the lift?'

'I shouldn't wonder.'

After this Peter felt happier about the shadowy passenger behind the bars. Father Christmas couldn't hurt anyone, even if he was (as Peter now believed him to be) his own father. Peter was only six but he could remember two Christmas Eves when his father had dressed up as Santa Claus and given him a delicious thrill. He could hardly wait for this one, when the apparition in the corner would at last become a reality.

Alas, two days before Christmas Day the lift broke down. On every floor it served, and there were five (six counting the basement), the forbidding notice 'Out of Order' dangled from the door handle. Peter complained as loudly as anyone, though secretly, he couldn't have told why, he was glad that the lift no longer functioned; and he didn't mind climbing the four flights to his room, which opened out of his parents' room but had its own door too. By using the stairs he met the workmen (he never knew on which floor they would be) and from them gleaned the latest news about the lift crisis. They were working overtime, they told him, and were just as anxious as he to see the last of the job. Sometimes they even told each other to put a jerk into it. Always Peter asked them when they would be finished, and they always answered, 'Christmas Eve at latest.'

Peter didn't doubt this. To him the workmen were infallible, possessed of magic powers capable of suspending the ordinary laws that governed lifts. Look how they left the gates open, and shouted to each other up and down the awesome lift shaft, paying as little attention to the other hotel visitors as if they didn't exist! Only to Peter did they vouchsafe a word.

But Christmas Eve came, the morning passed, the afternoon passed, and still the lift didn't go. The men were working with set faces and a controlled hurry in their movements; they didn't even return Peter's 'Good night' when he passed them on his way to bed. Bed! He had begged to be allowed to stay up this once for dinner; he knew he wouldn't go to sleep, he said, till Father Christmas came. He lay awake, listening to the urgent voices of the men, wondering if each hammer stroke would be the last; and then, just as the clamour was subsiding, he dropped off.

Dreaming, he felt adrift in time. Could it be midnight?

No, because his parents had after all consented to his going down to dinner. Now was the time. Averting his eyes from the forbidden lift he stole downstairs. There was a clock in the hall, but it had stopped. In the dining-room there was another clock; but dared he go into the dining-room alone, with no one to guide him and everybody looking at him?

He ventured in, and there, at their table, which he couldn't always pick out, he saw his mother. She saw him, too, and came towards him, threading her way between the tables as if they were just bits of furniture, not alien islands under hostile sway.

'Darling,' she said, 'I couldn't find you – nobody could, but here you are!' She led him back and they sat down. 'Daddy will be with us in a minute.' The minutes passed; suddenly there was a crash. It seemed to come from within, from the kitchen perhaps. Smiles lit up the faces of the diners. A man at a near by table laughed and said, 'Something's on the floor! Somebody'll be for it!'

'What is it?' whispered Peter, too excited to speak out loud. 'Is anyone hurt?'

'Oh, no, darling, somebody's dropped a tray, that's all.'

To Peter it seemed an anticlimax, this paltry accident that had stolen the thunder of his father's entry, for he didn't doubt that his father would come in as Father Christmas. The suspense was unbearable. 'Can I go into the hall and wait for him?' His mother hesitated and then said yes.

The hall was deserted, even the porter was off duty. Would it be fair, Peter wondered, or would it be cheating and doing himself out of a surprise, if he waited for Father Christmas by the lift? Magic has its rules which mustn't be disobeyed. But he was there now, at his old place in front of the lift; and the lift would come down if he pressed the button.

He knew he mustn't, that it was forbidden, that his father would be angry if he did; yet he reached up and pressed it.

But nothing happened, the lift didn't come, and why? Because some careless person had forgotten to shut the gates – 'monkeying with the lift', his father called it. Perhaps the workmen had forgotten, in their hurry to get home. There was only one thing to do – find out on which floor the gates had been left open, and then shut them.

On their own floor it was, and in his dream it didn't seem strange to Peter that the lift wasn't there, blocking the black hole of the lift shaft, though he daren't look down it. The gates clicked to. Triumph possessed him, triumph lent him wings; he was back on the ground floor, with his finger on the button. A thrill of power such as he had never known ran through him when the machinery answered to his touch.

But what was this? The lift was coming up from below, not down from above, and there was something wrong with its roof – a jagged hole that let the light through. But the figure was there in its accustomed corner, and this time it hadn't disappeared, it was still there, he could see it through the mazy crisscross of the bars, a figure in a red robe with white fur edges, and wearing a red cowl on its head: his father, Father Christmas, Daddy in the lift. But why didn't he look at Peter, and why was his white beard streaked with red?

The two grilles folded back when Peter pushed them. Toys were lying at his father's feet, but he couldn't touch them for they too were red, red and wet as the floor of the lift, red as the jag of lightning that tore through his brain . . .

The Visiting Star

ROBERT AICKMAN

The first time that Colvin, who had never been a frequent theatre-goer, ever heard of the great actress Arabella Rokeby, was when he was walking past the Hippodrome one night and Malnik, the manager of the Tabard Players, invited him into his office.

Had Colvin not been awarded a grant, remarkably insufficient for present prices, upon which to compose, collate, and generally scratch together a book upon the once thriving British industries of lead and plumbago mining, he would probably never have set eyes upon this bleak town. Tea was over (today it had been pilchard salad and chips); and Colvin had set out from the Emancipation Hotel, where he boarded, upon his regular evening walk. In fifteen or twenty minutes he would be beyond the gas lights, the granite setts, the nimbus of the pits. (Lead and plumbago mining had long been replaced by coal, as the town's main industry.) There had been no one else for tea and Mrs Royd had made it clear that the trouble he was causing had not passed unnoticed.

Outside it was blowing as well as raining, so that Palmerston Street was almost deserted. The Hippodrome (called, when built, the Grand Opera House) stood at the corner of Palmerston Street and Aberdeen Place. Vast, ornate, the product of an unfulfilled aspiration that the town would increase in size and devotion to the Muses, it had been for years unused and forgotten. About it like rags, when Colvin first beheld it, had hung scraps of posters: 'Harem Nights. Gay! Bright!! Alluring!!!' But a few weeks ago the Hippodrome had reopened to admit the Tabard Players ('In Association with the Arts Council'); and, it was hoped, their audiences. The Tabard Players offered soberer joys: a new and respectable play each week, usually a light comedy or West End crook drama; but, on one occasion, *Everyman*. Malnik, their manager, a youngish bald man, was an authority on the British Drama of the Nineteenth Century, upon which he had written an immense book, bursting with carefully verified detail. Colvin had met him one night in the saloon bar of the Emancipation Hotel; and, though neither knew anything of the other's subject, they had exchanged cultural lifebelts in the ocean of apathy and incomprehensible interests which surrounded them. Malnik was lodging with the sad-faced Rector, who let rooms.

Tonight, having seen the curtain up on Act I, Malnik had come outside for a breath of the wind. There was something he wanted to impart, and, as he regarded the drizzling and indifferent town, Colvin obligingly came into sight. In a moment, he was inside Malnik's roomy but crumbling office.

'Look,' said Malnik.

He shuffled a heap of papers on his desk and handed Colvin a photograph. It was yellow, and torn at the edges. The subject was a wild-eyed young man with much dark curly hair and a blobby face. He was wearing a high stiff collar, and a bow like Chopin's.

'John Nethers,' said Malnik. Then, when no light of rapture flashed from Colvin's face, he said, 'Author of *Cornelia*.'

'Sorry,' said Colvin, shaking his head.

'John Nethers was the son of a chemist in this town. Some books say a miner, but that's wrong. A chemist. He killed himself at twenty-two. But before that I've traced that he'd written at least six plays. *Cornelia*, which is the best of them, is one of the great plays of the nineteenth century.'

'Why did he kill himself?'

'It's in his eyes. You can see it. *Cornelia* was produced

in London with Arabella Rokeby. But never here. Never in the author's own town. I've been into the whole thing closely. Now we're going to do *Cornelia* for Christmas.'

'Won't you lose money?' asked Colvin.

'We're losing money all the time, old man. Of course we are. We may as well do something we shall be remembered by.'

Colvin nodded. He was beginning to see that Malnik's life was a single-minded struggle for the British Drama of the Nineteenth Century and all that went with it.

'Besides I'm going to do *As You Like It* also. As a fill-up.' Malnik stooped and spoke close to Colvin's ear as he sat in a bursting leather armchair, the size of a Judge's seat. 'You see, Arabella Rokeby's *coming*.'

'But how long is it since—'

'Better not be too specific about that. They say it doesn't matter with Arabella Rokeby. She can get away with it. Probably in fact she can't. Not altogether. But all the same, think of it. Arabella Rokeby in *Cornelia*. In *my* theatre.'

Colvin thought of it.

'Have you ever seen her?'

'No, I haven't. Of course she doesn't play regularly nowadays. Only special engagements. But in this business one has to take a chance sometimes. And golly what a chance!'

'And she's willing to come? I mean at Christmas,' Colvin added, not wishing to seem rude.

Malnik did seem slightly unsure. 'I have a contract,' he said. Then he added: 'She'll love it when she gets here. After all: *Cornelia*! And she must know that the nineteenth-century theatre is my subject.' He had seemed to be reassuring himself, but now he was glowing.

'But *As You Like It*?' said Colvin, who had played Touchstone at his preparatory school. 'Surely she can't manage Rosalind?'

'It was her great part. Happily you can play Rosalind at any age. Wish I could get old Ludlow to play Jaques. But he won't.' Ludlow was the company's veteran.

'Why not?'

'He played with Rokeby in the old days. I believe he's afraid she'll see he isn't the Grand Old Man he should be. He's a good chap, but proud. Of course he may have other reasons. You never know with Ludlow.'

The curtain was down on Act I.

Colvin took his leave and resumed his walk.

~

Shortly thereafter Colvin read about the Nethers Gala in the local evening paper ('this forgotten poet', as the writer helpfully phrased it), and found confirmation that Miss Rokeby was indeed to grace it ('the former London star').

In the same issue of the paper appeared an editorial to the effect that widespread disappointment would be caused by the news that the Hippodrome would not be offering a pantomime at Christmas in accordance with the custom of the town and district.

'She can't 'ardly stop 'ere, Mr Colvin,' said Mrs Royd, when Colvin, thinking to provide forewarning, showed her the news, as she lent a hand behind the saloon bar. 'This isn't the Cumberland. She'd get across the staff.'

'I believe she's quite elderly,' said Colvin soothingly.

'If she's elderly, she'll want special attention, and that's often just as bad.'

'After all, where she goes is mainly a problem for her, and perhaps Mr Malnik.'

'Well, there's nowhere else in town for her to stop, is there?' retorted Mrs Royd with fire. 'Not nowadays. She'll just 'ave to make do. We did for theatricals in the old days. Midgets once. Whole troupe of 'em.'

'I'm sure you'll make her very comfortable.'

'Can't see what she wants to come at all for, really. Not at Christmas.'

'Miss Rokeby needs no *reason* for her actions. What she does is sufficient in itself. You'll understand that, dear lady, when you meet her.' The speaker was a very small man, apparently of advanced years, white-haired, and with a brown sharp face, like a Levantine. The bar was full, and Colvin had not previously noticed him, although he was conspicuous enough, as he wore an overcoat with a fur collar and a scarf with a large black pin in the centre. 'I wonder if I could beg a room for a few nights,' he went on. 'I assure you I'm no trouble at all.'

'There's only Number Twelve A. It's not very comfortable,' replied Mrs Royd sharply.

'Of course you must leave room for Miss Rokeby.'

'Nine's for her. Though I haven't had a word from her.'

'I think she'll need two rooms. She has a companion.'

'I can clear out Greta's old room upstairs. If she's a friend of yours, you might ask her to let me know when she's coming.'

'Not a friend,' said the old man, smiling. 'But I follow her career.'

Mrs Royd brought a big red book from under the bar.

'What name, please?'

'Mr Superbus,' said the little old man. He had yellow, expressionless eyes.

'Will you register?'

Mr Superbus produced a gold pen, long and fat. His writing was so curvilinear that it seemed purely decorative, like a design for ornamental ironwork. Colvin noticed that he paused slightly at the 'Permanent Address' column, and then simply wrote (although it was difficult to be sure) what appeared to be 'North Africa'.

'Will you come this way?' said Mrs Royd, staring suspiciously at the newcomer's scrollwork in the visitor's book. Then, even more suspiciously, she added: 'What about luggage?'

Mr Superbus nodded gravely. 'I placed two bags outside.'

'Let's hope they're still there. They're rough in this town, you know.'

'I'm sure they're still there,' said Mr Superbus.

As he spoke the door opened suddenly and a customer almost fell into the bar. 'Sorry, Mrs Royd,' he said with a mildness which in the circumstances belied Mrs Royd's words. 'There's something on the step.'

'My fault, I'm afraid,' said Mr Superbus. 'I wonder – have you a porter?'

'The porter works evenings at the Hippodrome nowadays. Scene-shifting and that.'

'Perhaps I could help?' said Colvin.

On the step outside were what appeared to be two very large suitcases. When he tried to lift one of them, he understood what Mr Superbus had meant. It was remarkably heavy. He held back the bar door, letting in a cloud of cold air. 'Give me a hand someone,' he said.

The customer who had almost fallen volunteered, and a short procession, led by Mrs Royd, set off along the little dark passage to Number Twelve A. Colvin was disconcerted when he realised that Twelve A was the room at the end of the passage, which had no number on its door and had never, he thought, been occupied since his arrival; the room, in fact, next to his.

'Better leave these on the floor,' said Colvin, dismissing the rickety luggage stand.

'Thank you,' said Mr Superbus, transferring a coin to the man who had almost fallen. He did it like a conjuror unpalming something.

'I'll send Greta to make up the bed,' said Mrs Royd. 'Tea's at six.'

'At six?' said Mr Superbus, gently raising an eyebrow. 'Tea?' Then, when Mrs Royd and the man had gone, he clutched Colvin very hard on the upper part of his left arm. 'Tell me,' enquired Mr Superbus, 'are you in love with Miss Rokeby? I overheard you defending her against the impertinence of our hostess.'

Colvin considered for a moment.

'Why not admit it?' said Mr Superbus, gently raising the other eyebrow. He was still clutching Colvin's arm much too hard.

'I've never set eyes on Miss Rokeby.'

Mr Superbus let go. 'Young people nowadays have no imagination,' he said with a whinny, like a wild goat.

~

Colvin was not surprised when Mr Superbus did not appear for tea (pressed beef and chips that evening). After tea Colvin, instead of going for a walk, wrote to his mother. But there was little to tell her, so that at the end of the letter he mentioned the arrival of Mr Superbus. 'There's a sort of sweet blossomy smell about him like a meadow,' he ended. 'I think he must use scent.'

When the letter was finished, Colvin started trying to construct tables of output from the lead and plumbago mines a century ago. The partitions between the bedrooms were thin, and he began to wonder about Mr Superbus's nocturnal habits.

He wondered from time to time until the time came for sleep, and wondered a bit also as he dressed the next morning and went to the bathroom to shave. For during the whole of this time no sound whatever had been heard from Number Twelve A, despite the thinness of the plywood partition; a circumstance which Colvin already thought curious when, during breakfast, he overheard Greta talking to Mrs Royd in the kitchen. 'I'm ever so sorry, Mrs Royd. I forgot about it with the crowd in the bar.' To which Mrs Royd simply replied: 'I wonder what 'e done about it. 'E could 'ardly do without sheets or blankets, and this December. Why didn't 'e *ask*?' And when Greta said, 'I suppose nothing ain't happened to him?' Colvin put down his porridge

spoon and unobtrusively joined the party which went
to find out.

Mrs Royd knocked several times upon the door of
Number Twelve A, but there was no answer. When they
opened the door, the bed was bare as Colvin had seen it
the evening before, and there was no sign at all of Mr
Superbus except that his two big cases lay on the floor,
one beside the other.

'What's he want to leave the window open like that
for?' enquired Mrs Royd. She shut it with a crash. 'Someone
will fall over those cases in the middle of the floor.'

Colvin bent down to slide the heavy cases under the
bed. But the pair of them now moved at a touch.

Colvin picked one case up and shook it slightly. It
emitted a muffled flapping sound, like a bat in a box.
Colvin nearly spoke, but stopped himself and stowed the
cases, end on, under the unmade bed in silence.

'Make up the room, Greta,' said Mrs Royd. 'It's no
use just standing about.' Colvin gathered that it was not
altogether unknown for visitors to the Emancipation
Hotel to be missing from their rooms all night. But there
was a further little mystery. Later that day in the bar,
Colvin was accosted by the man who had helped to carry
Mr Superbus's luggage.

'Look at that.' He displayed, rather furtively, something
which lay in his hand.

It was a sovereign.

'He gave it me last night.'

'Can I see it?' It had been struck in Queen Victoria's reign, but gleamed like new.

'What d'you make of that?' asked the man.

'Not much,' replied Colvin, returning the pretty piece. 'But now I come to think of it, *you* can make about forty-five shillings.'

When this incident took place, Colvin was on his way to spend three or four nights in another town where lead and plumbago mining had formerly been carried on, and where he needed to consult an invaluable collection of old records which had been presented to the Public Library at the time the principal mining company went bankrupt.

On his return, he walked up the hill from the station through a thick mist, laden with coal dust and sticky smoke, and apparently in no way diminished by a bitter little wind, which chilled while hardly troubling to blow. There had been snow, and little archipelagos of slush remained on the pavements, through which the immense boots of the miners crashed noisily. The male population wore heavy mufflers and were unusually silent. Many of the women wore shawls over their heads in the manner of their grandmothers.

Mrs Royd was not in the bar, and Colvin hurried

through it to his old room, where he put on a thick sweater before descending to tea. The only company consisted in two commercial travellers, sitting at the same table and eating through a heap of bread and margarine but saying nothing. Colvin wondered what had happened to Mr Superbus.

Greta entered as usual with a pot of strong tea and a plate of bread and margarine.

'Good evening, Mr Colvin. Enjoy your trip?'

'Yes, thank you, Greta. What's for tea?'

'Haddock and chips.' She drew a deep breath. 'Miss Rokeby's come . . . I don't think she'll care for haddock and chips, do you, Mr Colvin?' Colvin looked up in surprise. He saw that Greta was trembling. Then he noticed that she was wearing a thin black dress, instead of her customary casual attire.

Colvin smiled up at her. 'I think you'd better put on something warm. It's getting colder every minute.'

But at that moment the door opened and Miss Rokeby entered.

Greta stood quite still, shivering all over, and simply staring at her. Everything about Greta made it clear that this was Miss Rokeby. Otherwise the situation was of a kind which brought to Colvin's mind the cliché about there being some mistake.

The woman who had come in was very small and

slight. She had a triangular gazelle-like face, with very large dark eyes, and a mouth which went right across the lower tip of the triangle, making of her chin another, smaller triangle. She was dressed entirely in black, with a high-necked black silk sweater, and wore long black earrings. Her short dark hair was dressed like that of a faun, and her thin white hands hung straight by her side in a posture resembling some Indian statuettes which Colvin recalled but could not place.

Greta walked towards her, and drew back a chair. She placed Miss Rokeby with her back to Colvin.

'Thank you. What can I eat?' Colvin was undecided whether Miss Rokeby's voice was high or low: it was like a bell beneath the ocean.

Greta was blushing. She stood, not looking at Miss Rokeby, but at the other side of the room, shivering and reddening. Then tears began to pour down her cheeks in a cataract. She dragged at a chair, made an unintelligible sound, and ran into the kitchen.

Miss Rokeby half turned in her seat, and stared after Greta. Colvin thought she looked quite as upset as Greta. Certainly she was very white. She might almost have been eighteen.

'Please don't mind. It's nerves, I think.' Colvin realised that his own voice was far from steady, and that he was beginning to blush also, he hoped only slightly.

Miss Rokeby had risen to her feet and was holding on to the back of her chair.

'I didn't say anything which could frighten her.'

It was necessary to come to the point, Colvin thought.

'Greta thinks the menu unworthy of the distinguished company.'

'What?' She turned and looked at Colvin. Then she smiled. 'Is that it?' She sat down again. 'What is it? Fish and chips?'

'Haddock. Yes.' Colvin smiled back, now full of confidence.

'Well. There it is.' Miss Rokeby made the prospect of haddock sound charming and gay. One of the commercial travellers offered to pour the other a fourth cup of tea. The odd little crisis was over.

But when Greta returned, her face seemed set and a trifle hostile. She had put on an ugly custard-coloured cardigan.

'It's haddock and chips.'

Miss Rokeby merely inclined her head, still smiling charmingly.

~

Before Colvin had finished, Miss Rokeby, with whom further conversation had been made difficult by the fact that she had been seated with her back to him, and by the torpid watchfulness of the commercial travellers, rose, bade him 'Good evening,' and left.

Colvin had not meant to go out again that evening, but curiosity continued to rise in him, and in the end he decided to clear his thoughts by a short walk, taking in the Hippodrome. Outside it had become even colder; the fog was thicker, the streets emptier.

Colvin found that the entrance to the Hippodrome had been transformed. From frieze to floor, the walls were covered with large photographs. The photographs were not framed, but merely mounted on big sheets of pasteboard. They seemed to be all the same size. Colvin saw at once that they were all portraits of Miss Rokeby.

The entrance hall was filled with fog, but the lighting within had been greatly reinforced since Colvin's last visit. Tonight the effect was mistily dazzling. Colvin began to examine the photographs. They depicted Miss Rokeby in the widest variety of costumes and make-up, although in no case was the name given of the play or character. In some Colvin could not see how he recognised her at all. In all she was alone. The number of the photographs, their uniformity of presentation, the bright swimming lights, the emptiness of the place (for the box office had shut) combined to make Colvin feel that he was dreaming. He put his hands before his eyes, inflamed by the glare and the fog. When he looked again, it was as if all the Miss Rokebys had been so placed that their gaze converged upon the spot where he stood. He closed his eyes tightly and began to feel his way to the door and the dimness of the street outside. Then there was a flutter of applause behind him; the evening's audience began to straggle out, grumbling at the weather, and Malnik was saying 'Hullo, old man. Nice to see you.'

Colvin gesticulated uncertainly. 'Did she bring them all with her?'

'Not a bit of it, old man. Millie found them when she opened up.'

'Where did she find them?'

'Just lying on the floor. In two whacking great parcels. Rokeby's agent, I suppose, though she appeared not to have one. Blest if I know, really. I myself could hardly shift one of the parcels, let alone two.'

Colvin felt rather frightened for a moment, but he only said: 'How do you like her?'

'Tell you when she arrives.'

'She's arrived.'

Malnik stared.

'Come back with me and see for yourself.'

Malnik seized Colvin's elbow. 'What's she look like?'

'Might be any age.'

All the time Malnik was bidding goodnight to patrons,

trying to appease their indignation at being brought out on such a night.

Suddenly the lights went, leaving only a pilot. It illumined a photograph of Miss Rokeby holding a skull.

'Let's go,' said Malnik. 'Lock up, Frank, will you?'

'You'll need a coat,' said Colvin.

'Lend me your coat, Frank.'

~

On the short cold walk to the Emancipation Hotel, Malnik said little. Colvin supposed that he was planning the encounter before him. Colvin did ask him whether he had ever heard of a Mr Superbus, but he hadn't.

Mrs Royd was, it seemed, in a thoroughly bad temper. To Colvin it appeared that she had been drinking, and that she was one whom drink soured rather than mellowed. 'I've got no one to send,' she snapped. 'You can go up yourself, if you like. Mr Colvin knows the way.' There was a roaring fire in the bar, which after the cold outside seemed very overheated.

Outside Number Nine, Colvin paused before knocking. Immediately he was glad he had done so, because inside were voices speaking very softly. All the evening he had been remembering Mr Superbus's reference to a 'companion'.

In dumb-show he tried to convey the situation to

Malnik, who peered at his efforts with a professional's dismissal of the amateur. Then Malnik produced a pocket-book, wrote in it, and tore out the page, which he thrust under Miss Rokeby's door. Having done this, he prepared to return with Colvin to the bar, and await a reply. Before they had taken three steps, however, the door was open, and Miss Rokeby was inviting them in.

To Colvin she said, 'We've met already,' though without enquiring his name.

Colvin felt gratified and at least equally pleased when he saw that the fourth person in the room was a tall, frail-looking girl with long fair hair drawn back into a tight bun. It was not the sort of companion he had surmised.

'This is Myrrha. We're never apart.'

Myrrha smiled slightly, said nothing, and sat down again. Colvin thought she looked positively wasted. Doubtless by reason of the cold, she wore heavy tweeds, which went oddly with her air of fragility.

'How well do you know the play?' asked Malnik at the earliest possible moment.

'Well enough not to play in it.' Colvin saw Malnik turn grey. 'Since you've got me here, I'll play Rosalind. The rest was lies. Do you know,' she went on, addressing Colvin, 'that this man tried to trick me? You're not in the theatre, are you?'

Colvin, feeling embarrassed, smiled and shook his head.

'*Cornelia* is a masterpiece,' said Malnik furiously. 'Nethers was a genius.'

Miss Rokeby simply said 'Was' very softly, and seated herself on the arm of Myrrha's armchair, the only one in the room. It was set before the old-fashioned gas fire.

'It's announced. Everyone's waiting for it. People are coming from London. They're even coming from Cambridge.'

Myrrha turned away her head from Malnik's wrath.

'I was told – Another English Classic. Not an outpouring by little Jack Nethers. I won't do it.'

'*As You Like It* is only a fill-up. What more is it ever? *Cornelia* is the whole point of the Gala. Nethers was *born* in this town. Don't you understand?'

Malnik was so much in earnest that Colvin felt sorry for him. But even Colvin doubted whether Malnik's was the best way to deal with Miss Rokeby.

'Please play for me. Please.'

'Rosalind only.' Miss Rokeby was swinging her legs. They were young and lovely. There was more than one thing about this interview which Colvin did not care for.

'We'll talk it over in my office tomorrow.' Colvin identified this as a customary admission of defeat.

'This is a horrid place, isn't it?' said Miss Rokeby conversationally to Colvin.

'I'm used to it,' said Colvin, smiling. 'Mrs Royd has her softer side.'

'She's put poor Myrrha in a cupboard.'

Colvin remembered about Greta's old room upstairs.

'Perhaps she'd like to change rooms with me? I've been away and haven't even unpacked. It would be easy.'

'How kind you are! To that silly little girl! To me! And now to Myrrha! May I see?'

'Of course.'

Colvin took her into the passage. It seemed obvious that Myrrha would come also, but she did not. Apparently she left it to Miss Rokeby to dispose of her. Malnik sulked behind also.

Colvin opened the door of his room and switched on the light. Lying on his bed and looking very foolish was his copy of Bull's *Graphite and Its Uses*. He glanced round for Miss Rokeby. Then for the second time that evening, he felt frightened.

Miss Rokeby was standing in the ill-lit passage, just outside his doorway. It was unpleasantly apparent that she was terrified. Formerly pale, she was now quite white. Her hands were clenched, and she was breathing unnaturally deeply. Her big eyes were half shut, and to Colvin it seemed that it was something she *smelt* which was frightening her. This impression was so strong that he sniffed the chilly air himself once or twice, unavailingly.

Then he stepped forward, and his arms were around Miss Rokeby, who was palpably about to faint. Immediately Miss Rokeby was in his arms, such emotion swept through him as he had never before known. For what seemed a long moment, he was lost in the wonder of it. Then he was recalled by something which frightened him more than anything else, though for less reason. There was a sharp sound from Number Twelve A. Mr Superbus must have returned.

Colvin supported Miss Rokeby back to Number Nine. Upon catching sight of her, Myrrha gave a small but jarring cry, and helped her on to the bed.

'It's my heart,' said Miss Rokeby. 'My absurd heart.'

Malnik now looked more black than grey. 'Shall we send for a doctor?' he enquired, hardly troubling to mask the sarcasm.

Miss Rokeby shook her head once. It was the sibling gesture to her nod.

'Please don't trouble about moving,' she said to Colvin.

Colvin, full of confusion, looked at Myrrha, who was being resourceful with smelling salts.

'Goodnight,' said Miss Rokeby, softly but firmly. And as Colvin followed Malnik out of the room, she touched his hand.

~

Colvin passed the night almost without sleep, which was another new experience for him. A conflict of feelings about Miss Rokeby, all of them strong, was one reason for insomnia: another was the sequence of sounds from Number Twelve A. Mr Superbus seemed to spend the night in moving things about and talking to himself. At first it sounded as if he were rearranging all the furniture in his room. Then there was a period, which seemed to Colvin timeless, during which the only noise was of low and unintelligible muttering, by no means continuous, but broken by periods of silence and then resumed as before just as Colvin was beginning to hope that all was over. Colvin wondered whether Mr Superbus was saying his prayers. Ultimately the banging about recommenced. Presumably Mr Superbus was still dissatisfied with the arrangement of the furniture; or perhaps was returning it to its original dispositions. Then Colvin heard the sash window thrown sharply open. He remembered the sound from the occasion when Mrs Royd had sharply shut it. After that silence continued. In the end Colvin turned on the light and looked at his watch. It had stopped.

At breakfast, Colvin asked when Mr Superbus was expected down. 'He doesn't come down,' replied Greta. 'They say he has all his meals out.'

Colvin understood that rehearsals began that day, but

Malnik had always demurred at outsiders being present.
Now, moreover, he felt that Colvin had seen him at an
unfavourable moment, so that his cordiality was much
abated. The next two weeks, in fact, were to Colvin heavy
with anticlimax. He saw Miss Rokeby only at the evening
meal, which, however, she was undeniably in process of
converting from tea to dinner, by expending charm, will-
power, and cash. Colvin participated in this improvement,
as did even such few of the endless commercial travellers
as wished to do so; and from time to time Miss Rokeby
exchanged a few pleasant generalities with him, though
she did not ask him to sit at her table, nor did he, being
a shy man, dare to invite her. Myrrha never appeared at
all, and when on one occasion Colvin referred to her
interrogatively, Miss Rokeby simply said, 'She pines, poor
lamb,' and plainly wished to say nothing more. Colvin
remembered Myrrha's wasted appearance, and concluded
that she must be an invalid. He wondered if he should
again offer to change rooms. After that single disturbed
night, he had heard no more of Mr Superbus. But from
Mrs Royd he had gathered that Mr Superbus had settled
for several weeks in advance. Indeed, for the first time
in years the Emancipation Hotel was doing good business.

It continued as cold as ever during all the time Miss
Rokeby remained in the town, with repeated little snow
storms every time the streets began to clear. The miners

would stamp as they entered the bar until they seemed likely to go through to the cellar beneath; and all the commercial travellers caught colds. The two local papers, morning and evening, continued their efforts to set people against Malnik's now diminished Gala. When *Cornelia* was no longer offered, the two editors pointed out (erroneously, Colvin felt) that even now it was not too late for a pantomime: but Malnik seemed to have succeeded in persuading Miss Rokeby to reinforce *As You Like It* with a piece entitled *A Scrap of Paper* which Colvin had never heard of, but which an elderly local citizen whom the papers always consulted upon matters theatrical described as 'very old-fashioned'. Malnik caused further comment by proposing to open on Christmas Eve, when the unfailing tradition had been Boxing Night.

The final week of rehearsal was marred by an exceedingly distressing incident. It happened on the Tuesday. Coming in that morning from a cold visit to the Technical Institute Library, Colvin found in the stuffy little saloon bar a number of the Tabard Players. The Players usually patronised an establishment nearer to the Hippodrome; and the fact that the present occasion was out of the ordinary was emphasised by the demeanour of the group, who were clustered together and talking in low, serious voices. Colvin knew none of the players at all well, but the group looked so distraught that, partly from curiosity and partly from compassion, he ventured to enquire of one of them, a middle-aged actor named Shillitoe to whom Malnik had introduced him, what was the matter. After a short silence, the group seemed collectively to decide upon accepting Colvin among them, and all began to enlighten him in short strained bursts of over-eloquence. Some of the references were not wholly clear to Colvin, but the substance of the story was simple.

Colvin gathered that when the Tabard Players took possession of the Hippodrome, Malnik had been warned that the 'grid' above the stage was undependable, and that scenery should not be 'flown' from it. This restriction had caused grumbling, but had been complied with until, during a rehearsal of *A Scrap of Paper*, the producer had rebelled and asked Malnik for authority to use the grid. Malnik had agreed; and two stagehands began gingerly to pull on some of the dusty lines which disappeared into the almost complete darkness far above. Before long one of them had cried out that there was 'something up there already'. At these words, Colvin was told, everyone in the theatre fell silent. The stagehand went on paying out line, but the stage was so ample and the grid so high that an appreciable time passed before the object came slowly into view.

The narrators stopped, and there was a silence which Colvin felt must have been like the silence in the theatre.

Then Shillitoe resumed: 'It was poor old Ludlow's body. He'd hanged himself right up under the grid. Eighty feet above the floor of the stage. Some time ago, too. He wasn't in the Christmas plays, you know. Or in this week's play. We all thought he'd gone home.'

Colvin learnt that the producer had fainted right away; and, upon tactful enquiry, that Miss Rokeby had fortunately not been called for that particular rehearsal.

~

On the first two Sundays after her arrival, Miss Rokeby had been no more in evidence than on any other day, but on the morning of the third Sunday Colvin was taking one of his resolute lonely walks across the windy fells which surrounded the town when he saw her walking ahead of him through the snow. The snow lay only an inch or two deep upon the hillside ledge along which the path ran, and Colvin had been wondering for some time about the small footsteps which preceded him. It was the first time he had seen Miss Rokeby outside the Emancipation Hotel, but he had no doubt that it was she he saw, and his heart turned over at the sight. He hesitated, then walked faster, and soon had overtaken her. As he drew near, she stopped, turned, and faced him. Then, when she saw who it was, she seemed unsurprised. She wore a fur coat with a collar which reached almost to the tip of her nose, a fur hat and elegant boots which laced to the knee.

'I'm glad to have a companion,' she said gravely, sending Colvin's thoughts to her other odd companion. 'I suppose you know all these paths well?'

'I come up here often to look for lead workings. I'm writing a dull book on lead and plumbago mining.'

'I don't see any mines up here.' She looked around with an air of grave bewilderment.

'Lead mines aren't like coal mines. They're simply passages in hillsides.'

'What do you do when you find them?'

'I mark them on a large scale map. Sometimes I go down them.'

'Don't the miners object?'

'There are no miners.'

A shadow crossed her face.

'I mean, not any longer. We don't mine lead any more.'

'Don't we? Why not?'

'That's a complicated story.'

She nodded. 'Will you take me down a mine?'

'I don't think you'd like it. The passages are usually both narrow and low. One of the reasons why the industry's come to an end is that people would no longer work in them. Besides, now the mines are disused, they're often dangerous.'

She laughed. It was the first time he had ever heard her do so. 'Come on.' She took hold of his arm. 'Or aren't there any mines on this particular hillside?' She looked as concerned as a child.

'There's one about a hundred feet above our heads. But there's nothing to see. Only darkness.'

'Only *darkness*,' cried Miss Rokeby. She implied that no reasonable person could want more. 'But you don't go down all these passages only to see darkness?'

'I take a flashlight.'

'Have you got it now?'

'Yes.' Colvin never went to the fells without it.

'Then that will look after *you*. Where's the mine? Conduct me.'

They began to scramble together up the steep snow-covered slope. Colvin knew all the workings round here, and soon they were in the entry.

'You see,' said Colvin. 'There's not even room to stand, and a fat person couldn't get in at all. You'll ruin your coat.'

'I'm not a fat person.' There was a small excited patch in each of her cheeks. 'But you'd better go first.'

Colvin knew that this particular working consisted simply in a long passage, following the vein of lead. He had been to the end of it more than once. He turned on his flashlight. 'I assure you, there's nothing to see,' he said. And in he went.

Colvin perceived that Miss Rokeby seemed indeed to pass along the adit without even stooping or damaging her fur hat. She insisted on going as far as possible, although near the end Colvin made a quite strenuous effort to persuade her to let them return.

'What's that?' enquired Miss Rokeby when they had nonetheless reached the extremity of the passage.

'It's a big fault in the limestone. A sort of cave. The miners chucked their debris down it.'

'Is it deep?'

'Some of these faults are supposed to be bottomless.'

She took the light from his hand, and, squatting down on the brink of the hole, flashed it round the depths below.

'Careful,' cried Colvin. 'You're on loose shale. It could easily slip.' He tried to drag her back. The only result was that she dropped the flashlight, which went tumbling down the great hole like a meteor, until after many seconds they heard a faint crash. They were in complete darkness.

'I'm sorry,' said Miss Rokeby's voice. 'But you did push me.'

Trying not to fall down the hole, Colvin began to grope his way back. Suddenly he had thought of Malnik, and the irresponsibility of the proceedings upon which he was engaged appalled him. He begged Miss Rokeby to go slowly, test every step, and mind her head; but her unconcern seemed complete. Colvin tripped and toiled along for an endless period of time, with Miss Rokeby always close behind him, calm, sure of foot, and unflagging. As far into the earth as this, it was both warm and stuffy. Colvin began to fear that bad air might overcome them, forced as they were to creep so laboriously and interminably. He broke out in heavy perspiration.

Suddenly he knew that he would have to stop. He could not even pretend that it was out of consideration for Miss Rokeby. He subsided upon the floor of the passage and she seated herself near him, oblivious of her costly clothes. The blackness was still complete.

'Don't feel unworthy,' said Miss Rokeby softly. 'And don't feel frightened. There's no need. We shall get out.'

Curiously enough, the more she said, the worse Colvin felt. The strange antecedents to this misadventure were with him and, even more so, Miss Rokeby's whole fantastic background. He had to force his spine against the stone wall of the passage if he were not to give way to panic utterly and leap up screaming. Normal speech was impossible.

'Is it me you are frightened of?' asked Miss Rokeby, with dreadful percipience.

Colvin was less than ever able to speak.

'Would you like to know more about me?'

Colvin was shaking his head in the dark.

'If you'll promise not to tell anyone else.'

But, in fact, she was like a child, unable to contain her secret.

'I'm sure you won't tell anyone else . . . It's my helper. He's the queer one. Not me.'

Now that the truth was spoken Colvin felt a little better. 'Yes,' he said in a low, shaken voice, 'I know.'

'Oh, you know . . . *I* don't see him or –' she paused – 'or encounter him, often for years at a time. Years.'

'But you encountered him the other night?'

He could feel her shudder. 'Yes . . . You've seen him?'

'Very briefly . . . How did you . . . encounter him first?'

'It was years ago. Have you any idea how many years?'

'I think so.'

Then she said something which Colvin never really understood; not even later, in his dreams of her. 'You know I'm not here at all, really. Myrrha's me. That's why she's called Myrrha. That's how I act.'

'How?' said Colvin. There was little else to say.

'My helper took my own personality out of me. Like taking a nerve out of a tooth. Myrrha's my personality.'

'Do you mean your soul?' asked Colvin.

'Artists don't have souls,' said Miss Rokeby. 'Personality's the word . . . I'm anybody's personality. Or everybody's. And when I lost my personality, I stopped growing older, Of course I have to look after Myrrha, because if anything happened to Myrrha – well, you do see,' she continued.

'But Myrrha looks as young as you do.'

'That's what she *looks*.'

Colvin remembered Myrrha's wasted face.

'But how can you live without a personality? Besides,' added Colvin, 'you seem to me to have a very strong personality.'

'I have a mask for every occasion.'

It was only the utter blackness, Colvin felt, which made this impossible conversation possible.

'What do you do in exchange? I suppose you must repay your helper in some way?'

'I suppose I must . . . I've never found out what way it is.'

'What else does your helper do for you?'

'He smooths my path. Rids me of people who want to hurt me. He rid me of little Jack Nethers. Jack was mad, you know. You can see it even in his photograph.'

'Did he rid you of this wretched man Ludlow?'

'I don't know. You see, I can't remember Ludlow. I think he often rids me of people that I don't know want to hurt me.'

Colvin considered.

'Can you be rid of him?'

'I've never really tried.'

'Don't you *want* to be rid of him?'

'I don't know. He frightens me terribly whenever I come near him, but otherwise . . . I don't know. But for him I should never have been down a lead mine.'

'How many people know all this?' asked Colvin after a pause.

'Not many. I only told you because I wanted you to stop being frightened.'

As she spoke the passage was filled with a strange sound. Then they were illumined with icy December sunshine. Colvin perceived that they were almost at the entry to the working, and supposed that the portal must have been temporarily blocked by a miniature avalanche of melting snow. Even now there was, in fact, only a comparatively small hole, through which they would have to scramble.

'I told you we'd get out,' said Miss Rokeby. 'Other people haven't believed a word I said. But now *you'll* believe me.'

~

Not the least strange thing was the matter-of-fact manner in which, all the way back, Miss Rokeby questioned Colvin about his researches into lead and plumbago mining, with occasionally, on the perimeter of their talk, flattering enquiries about himself; although equally strange, Colvin considered, was the matter-of-fact manner in which he answered her. Before they were back in the town he was wondering how much of what she had said in the darkness of the mine had been meant only figuratively; and after that he wondered whether Miss Rokeby had not used the circumstances to initiate an imaginative and ingenious boutade. After all, he reflected, she was an actress. Colvin's hypothesis was, if anything, confirmed when at their parting she held his hand for a moment and said: 'Remember! *No one.*'

But he resolved to question Mrs Royd in a businesslike way about Mr Superbus. An opportunity arose when he encountered her after luncheon (at which Miss Rokeby had not made an appearance), reading *The People* before the fire in the saloon bar. The bar had just closed, and it was, Mrs Royd explained, the only warm spot in the house. In fact it was, as usual, hot as a kiln.

'Couldn't say, I'm sure,' replied Mrs Royd to Colvin's firm enquiry, and implying that it was neither her business nor his. 'Anyway, 'e's gone. Went last Tuesday. Didn't you notice, with 'im sleeping next to you?'

~

After the death of poor Ludlow (the almost inevitable verdict was suicide while of unsound mind), it was as if the papers felt embarrassed about continuing to carp at Malnik's plans, and by the opening night the editors seemed ready to extend the Christmas spirit even to Shakespeare. Colvin had planned to spend Christmas with his mother, but when he learned that Malnik's first night was to be on Christmas Eve, had been unable to resist deferring his departure until after it, despite the perils of a long and intricate railway journey on Christmas Day. With Miss Rokeby, however, he now felt entirely unsure of himself.

On Christmas Eve the town seemed full of merriment. Colvin was surprised at the frankness of the general rejoicing. The shops, as is usual in industrial districts, had long been offsetting the general drabness with drifts of Christmas cards and whirlpools of tinsel. Now every home seemed to be decorated and all the shops to be proclaiming bonus distributions and bumper share-outs. Even the queues, which were a prominent feature of these celebrations, looked more sanguine, Colvin noticed, when he stood in one of them for about half an hour in order to send Miss Rokeby some flowers, as he felt the occasion demanded. By the time he set out for the Hippodrome, the more domestically-minded citizens were everywhere quietly toiling at preparations for the morrow's revels, but a wilder minority, rebellious or homeless, were inaugurating such a carouse at the Emancipation Hotel as really to startle the comparatively retiring Colvin. He suspected that some of the bibbers must be Irish.

Sleet was slowly descending as Colvin stepped out of the sweltering bar in order to walk to the Hippodrome. A spot of it sailed gently into the back of his neck, chilling him in a moment. But, notwithstanding the weather, notwithstanding the claims of the season and the former attitude of the Press, there was a crowd outside the Hippodrome such as Colvin had never previously seen there. To his great surprise, some of the audience were in evening dress; many of them had expensive cars, and one party, it appeared, had come in a closed carriage with two flashing black horses. There was such a concourse at the doors that Colvin had to stand a long time in the slowly falling sleet before he was able to join the throng which forced its way, like icing onto a cake, between the countless glittering photographs of beautiful Miss Rokeby. The average age of the audience, Colvin observed, seemed very advanced, and especially of that section of it which was in evening dress. Elderly white-haired men with large noses and carnations in their buttonholes spoke in elegant Edwardian voices to the witchlike ladies on their arms, most of whom wore hothouse gardenias.

Inside, however, the huge and golden Hippodrome looked as it was intended to look when it was still named the Grand Opera House. From his gangway seat in the stalls Colvin looked backwards and upwards at the gilded satyrs and bacchantes who wantoned on the dress-circle balustrade, and at the venerable and orchidaceous figures who peered above them. The small orchestra was frenziedly playing selections from *L'Étoile du Nord*. In the gallery distant figures, unable to find seats, were standing watchfully. Even the many boxes, little used and dusty, were filling up. Colvin could only speculate how this gratifying assembly had been collected. But then he was on his feet for the national anthem, and the faded crimson and gold curtain, made deceivingly splendid by the footlights, was about to rise.

The play began, and then: 'Dear Celia, I show more mirth than I am mistress of, and would you yet I were merrier? Unless you could teach me to forget a banished father, you must not learn me how to remember any extraordinary pleasure.'

Colvin realised that in his heart he had expected Miss Rokeby to be good, to be moving, to be lovely, but the revelation he now had was something he could never have expected because he could never have imagined it, and before the conclusion of Rosalind's first scene in boy's attire in the Forest, he was wholly and terribly bewitched.

No one coughed, no one rustled, no one moved. To Colvin, it seemed as if Miss Rokeby's magic had strangely enchanted the normally journeyman Tabard Players into miracles of judgment. Plainly her spell was on the audience also, so that when the lights came up for the interval, Colvin found that his eyes were streaming, and felt not chagrin, but pride.

The interval was an uproar. Even the bells of fire engines pounding through the wintry night outside could hardly be heard above the din. People spoke freely to unknown neighbours, groping to express forgotten emotions. 'What a prelude to Christmas!' everyone said. Malnik was proved right in one thing.

During the second half, Colvin, failing of interest in Sir Oliver Martext's scene, let his eyes wander round the auditorium. He noticed that the nearest dress-circle box, previously unoccupied, appeared to be unoccupied no longer. A hand, which, being only just above him, he could see was gnarled and hirsute, was tightly gripping the box's red velvet curtain. Later in the scene between Silvius and Phebe (Miss Rokeby having come and gone meanwhile), the hand was still there, and still gripping tightly, as it was (after Rosalind's big scene with Orlando) during the Forester's song. At the beginning of Act V, there was a rush of feet down the gangway, and someone was crouching by Colvin's seat. It was Greta. 'Mr Colvin! There's been a fire. Miss Rokeby's friend jumped out of the window. She's terribly hurt. Will you tell Miss Rokeby?'

'The play's nearly over,' said Colvin. 'Wait for me at the back.' Greta withdrew, whimpering.

After Rosalind's Epilogue the tumult was millennial. Miss Rokeby, in Rosalind's white dress, stood for many seconds not bowing but quite still and unsmiling, with her hands by her sides as Colvin had first seen her. Then as the curtain rose and revealed the rest of the company, she began slowly to walk backwards upstage. Door keepers and even stagehands, spruced up for the purpose, began to bring armfuls upon armfuls of flowers, until there was a heap, a mountain of them in the centre of the stage, so high that it concealed Miss Rokeby's small figure from the audience. Suddenly a bouquet flew through the air from the dress-circle box. It landed at the very front of the heap. It was a hideous dusty laurel wreath, adorned with an immense and somewhat tasteless purple bow. The audience were yelling for Miss Rokeby like Dionysians, and the company, flagging from unaccustomed emotional expenditure, and plainly much scared, were looking for her, but in the end the stage manager had to lower the Safety Curtain and give orders that the house be cleared.

~

Back at the Emancipation Hotel, Colvin, although he had little title, asked to see the body.

'You wouldn't ever recognise her,' said Mrs Royd. Colvin did not pursue the matter.

The snow, falling ever more thickly, had now hearsed the town in silence.

'She didn't 'ave to do it,' wailed on Mrs Royd. 'The brigade had the flames under control. And tomorrow Christmas Day!'

Nicholas Was

NEIL GAIMAN

Nicholas Was . . .

older than sin, and his beard could grow no whiter. He wanted to die.

The dwarfish natives of the Arctic caverns did not speak his language, but conversed in their own, twittering tongue, conducted incomprehensible rituals, when they were not actually working in the factories.

Once every year they forced him, sobbing and protesting, into Endless Night. During the journey he would stand near every child in the world, leave one of the dwarves' invisible gifts by its bedside. The children slept, frozen into time.

He envied Prometheus and Loki, Sisyphus and Judas. His punishment was harsher.

Ho.

Ho.

Ho.

The Ghost of the Blue Chamber

JEROME K. JEROME

THE GHOST OF THE BLUE CHAMBER

(My Uncle's Story)

'I don't want to make you fellows nervous,' began my uncle in a peculiarly impressive, not to say blood-curdling, tone of voice, 'and if you would rather that I did not mention it, I won't; but, as a matter of fact, this very house, in which we are now sitting, is haunted.'

'You don't say that!' exclaimed Mr Coombes.

'What's the use of your saying I don't say it when I have just said it?' retorted my uncle somewhat pettishly. 'You do talk so foolishly. I tell you the house is haunted. Regularly on Christmas Eve the Blue Chamber [they called the room next to the nursery the 'blue chamber', at my uncle's, most of the toilet service being of that shade] is haunted by the ghost of a sinful man – a man who once killed a Christmas wait with a lump of coal.'

'How did he do it?' asked Mr Coombes, with eager anxiousness. 'Was it difficult?'

'I do not know how he did it,' replied my uncle, 'he did not explain the process. The wait had taken up a position just inside the front gate, and was singing a ballad. It is presumed that, when he opened his mouth for B flat, the lump of coal was thrown by the sinful man from one of the windows, and that it went down the wait's throat and choked him.'

'You want to be a good shot, but it is certainly worth trying,' murmured Mr Coombes thoughtfully.

'But that was not his only crime, alas!' added my uncle. 'Prior to that he had killed a solo cornet player.'

'No! Is that really a fact?' exclaimed Mr Coombes.

'Of course it's a fact,' answered my uncle testily, 'at all events, as much a fact as you can expect to get in a case of this sort.

'How very captious you are this evening. The circumstantial evidence was overwhelming. The poor fellow, the cornet player, had been in the neighbourhood barely a month. Old Mr Bishop, who kept the "Jolly Sand Boys" at the time, and from whom I had the story, said he had never known a more hard-working and energetic solo cornet player. He, the cornet player, only knew two tunes, but Mr Bishop said that the man could not have played with more vigour, or for more hours in a day, if he had known forty. The two tunes he did play were "Annie Laurie" and "Home, Sweet Home"; and as regarded his performance of the former melody, Mr Bishop said that a mere child could have told what it was meant for.

'This musician – this poor, friendless artist used to come regularly and play in this street just opposite for two hours every evening. One evening he was seen, evidently in response to an invitation, going into this very house, BUT WAS NEVER SEEN COMING OUT OF IT!'

'Did the townsfolk try offering any reward for his recovery?' asked Mr Coombes.

'Not a ha'penny,' replied my uncle.

'Another summer,' continued my uncle, 'a German band visited here, intending – so they announced on their arrival – to stay till the autumn.

'On the second day from their arrival, the whole company, as fine and healthy a body of men as one could wish to see, were invited to dinner by this sinful man, and, after spending the whole of the next twenty-four hours in bed, left the town a broken and dyspeptic crew; the parish doctor, who had attended them, giving it as his opinion that it was doubtful if they would, any of them, be fit to play an air again.'

'You – you don't know the recipe, do you?' asked Mr Coombes.

'Unfortunately I do not,' replied my uncle; 'but the chief ingredient was said to have been railway refreshment-room pork pie.

'I forget the man's other crimes,' my uncle went on, 'I used to know them all at one time, but my memory is not what it was. I do not, however, believe I am doing his memory an injustice in believing that he was not entirely unconnected with the death, and subsequent burial, of a gentleman who used to play the harp with his toes; and that neither was he altogether unresponsible for the lonely grave of an unknown stranger who had once visited the neighbourhood, an Italian peasant lad, a performer upon the barrel organ.

'Every Christmas Eve,' said my uncle, cleaving with low impressive tones the strange awed silence that, like a shadow, seemed to have slowly stolen into and settled down upon the room, 'the ghost of this sinful man haunts the Blue Chamber, in this very house. There, from midnight until cock-crow, amid wild muffled shrieks and groans and mocking laughter and the ghostly sound of horrid blows, it does fierce phantom fight with the spirits of the solo cornet player and the murdered wait, assisted at intervals, by the shades of the German band; while the ghost of the strangled harpist plays mad ghostly melodies with ghostly toes on the ghost of a broken harp.'

Uncle said the Blue Chamber was comparatively useless as a sleeping-apartment on Christmas Eve.

'Hark!' said uncle, raising a warning hand towards the ceiling, while we held our breath, and listened; 'Hark! I believe they are at it now – in the BLUE CHAMBER!'

THE BLUE CHAMBER

I rose up, and said that I would sleep in the Blue Chamber.

Before I tell you my own story, however – the story of what happened in the Blue Chamber – I would wish to preface it with:

A PERSONAL EXPLANATION

I feel a good deal of hesitation about telling you this story of my own. You see it is not a story like the other stories that I have been telling you, or rather that Teddy Biffles, Mr Coombes, and my uncle have been telling you: it is a true story. It is not a story told by a person sitting round a fire on Christmas Eve, drinking whisky punch: it is a record of events that actually happened.

Indeed, it is not a 'story' at all, in the commonly accepted meaning of the word: it is a report. It is, I feel, almost out of place in a book of this kind. It is more suitable to a biography, or an English history.

There is another thing that makes it difficult for me

to tell you this story, and that is, that it is all about myself. In telling you this story, I shall have to keep on talking about myself; and talking about ourselves is what we modern-day authors have a strong objection to doing. If we literary men of the new school have one praise-worthy yearning more ever present to our minds than another it is the yearning never to appear in the slightest degree egotistical.

I myself, so I am told, carry this coyness – this shrinking reticence concerning anything connected with my own personality, almost too far, and people grumble at me because of it. People come to me and say –

'Well, now, why don't you talk about yourself a bit? That's what we want to read about. Tell us something about yourself.'

But I have always replied, 'No.' It is not that I do not think the subject an interesting one. I cannot myself conceive of any topic more likely to prove fascinating to the world as a whole, or at all events to the cultured portion of it. But I will not do it, on principle. It is inartistic, and it sets a bad example to the younger men. Other writers (a few of them) do it, I know; but I will not – not as a rule.

Under ordinary circumstances, therefore, I should not tell you this story at all. I should say to myself, 'No! It is a good story, it is a moral story, it is a strange, weird, enthralling sort of a story, and the public, I know, would like to hear it, and I should like to tell it to them, but it is all about myself – about what I said, and what I saw, and what I did, and I cannot do it. My retiring, anti-egotistical nature will not permit me to talk in this way about myself.'

But the circumstances surrounding this story are not ordinary, and there are reasons prompting me, in spite of my modesty, to rather welcome the opportunity of relating it.

As I stated at the beginning, there has been unpleasantness in our family over this party of ours, and, as regards myself in particular, and my share in the events I am now about to set forth, gross injustice has been done me.

As a means of replacing my character in its proper light – of dispelling the clouds of calumny and misconception with which it has been darkened, I feel that my best course is to give a simple, dignified narration of the plain facts, and allow the unprejudiced to judge for themselves. My chief object, I candidly confess, is to clear myself from unjust aspersion. Spurred by this motive – and I think it is an honourable and a right motive – I find I am enabled to overcome my usual repugnance to talking about myself, and can thus tell:

MY OWN STORY

As soon as my uncle had finished his story, I, as I have already told you, rose up and said that *I* would sleep in the Blue Chamber that very night.

'Never!' cried my uncle, springing up. 'You shall not put yourself in this deadly peril. Besides, the bed is not made.'

'Never mind the bed,' I replied. 'I have lived in furnished apartments for gentlemen, and have been accustomed to sleep on beds that have never been made from one year's end to the other. Do not thwart me in my resolve. I am young, and have had a clear conscience now for over a month. The spirits will not harm me. I may even do them some little good, and induce them to be quiet and go away. Besides, I should like to see the show.'

Saying which, I sat down again. (How Mr Coombes came to be in my chair, instead of at the other side of the room, where he had been all the evening, and why he never offered to apologise when I sat right down on top of him, and why young Biffles should have tried to palm himself off upon me as my Uncle John, and induced me, under that erroneous impression, to shake him by the hand for nearly three minutes, and tell him that I had always regarded him as father, are matters that, to this day, I have never been able to fully understand.)

They tried to dissuade me from what they termed my

foolhardy enterprise, but I remained firm, and claimed my privilege. I was 'the guest'. 'The guest' always sleeps in the haunted chamber on Christmas Eve; it is his perquisite.

They said that if I put it on that footing, they had, of course, no answer, and they lighted a candle for me, and accompanied me upstairs in a body.

Whether elevated by the feeling that I was doing a noble action, or animated by a mere general consciousness of rectitude, is not for me to say, but I went upstairs that night with remarkable buoyancy. It was as much as I could do to stop at the landing when I came to it; I felt I wanted to go on up to the roof. But, with the help of the banisters, I restrained my ambition, wished them all goodnight, and went in and shut the door.

Things began to go wrong with me from the very first. The candle tumbled out of the candlestick before my hand was off the lock. It kept on tumbling out of the candlestick, and every time I picked, put it up and put it in, it tumbled out again: I never saw such a slippery candle. I gave up attempting to use the candlestick at last and carried the candle about in my hand, and, even then, it would not keep upright. So I got wild and threw it out of window, and undressed and went to bed in the dark.

I did not go to sleep, I did not feel sleepy at all, I lay

on my back, looking up at the ceiling, and thinking of things. I wish I could remember some of the ideas that came to me as I lay there, because they were so amusing. I laughed at them myself till the bed shook.

I had been lying like this for half an hour or so, and had forgotten all about the ghost, when, on casually casting my eyes round the room, I noticed for the first time a singularly contented-looking phantom, sitting in the easychair by the fire, smoking the ghost of a long clay pipe.

I fancied for the moment, as most people would under similar circumstances, that I must be dreaming. I sat up, and rubbed my eyes.

No! It was a ghost, clear enough. I could see the back of the chair through his body. He looked over towards me, took the shadowy pipe from his lips, and nodded.

The most surprising part of the whole thing to me was that I did not feel in the least alarmed. If anything, I was rather pleased to see him. It was company.

I said, 'Good evening. It's been a cold day!'

He said he had not noticed it himself, but dared say I was right.

We remained silent for a few seconds, and then, wishing to put it pleasantly, I said, 'I believe I have the honour of addressing the ghost of the gentleman who had the accident with the wait?'

He smiled, and said it was very good of me to remember it. One wait was not much to boast of, but still, every little helped.

I was somewhat staggered at his answer. I had expected a groan of remorse. The ghost appeared, on the contrary, to be rather conceited over the business. I thought that, as he had taken my reference to the wait so quietly, perhaps he would not be offended if I questioned him about the organ grinder. I felt curious about that poor boy.

'Is it true,' I asked, 'that you had a hand in the death of that Italian peasant lad who came to the town once with a barrel organ that played nothing but Scotch airs?'

He quite fired up. 'Had a hand in it!' he exclaimed indignantly. 'Who has dared to pretend that he assisted me? I murdered the youth myself. Nobody helped me. Alone I did it. Show me the man who says I didn't.'

I calmed him. I assured him that I had never, in my own mind, doubted that he was the real and only assassin, and I went on and asked him what he had done with the body of the cornet player he had killed.

He said, 'To which one may you be alluding?'

'Oh, were there any more then?' I inquired.

He smiled, and gave a little cough. He said he did not like to appear to be boasting, but that, counting trombones, there were seven.

'Dear me!' I replied, 'you must have had quite a busy time of it, one way and another.'

He said that perhaps he ought not to be the one to say so, but that really, speaking of ordinary middle-society, he thought there were few ghosts who could look back upon a life of more sustained usefulness.

He puffed away in silence for a few seconds, while I sat watching him. I had never seen a ghost smoking a pipe before, that I could remember, and it interested me.

I asked him what tobacco he used, and he replied, 'The ghost of cut cavendish, as a rule.'

He explained that the ghost of all the tobacco that a man smoked in life belonged to him when he became dead. He said he himself had smoked a good deal of cut cavendish when he was alive, so that he was well supplied with the ghost of it now.

I observed that it was a useful thing to know that, and I made up my mind to smoke as much tobacco as ever I could before I died.

I thought I might as well start at once, so I said I would join him in a pipe, and he said, 'Do, old man'; and I reached over and got out the necessary paraphernalia from my coat pocket and lit up.

We grew quite chummy after that, and he told me all his crimes. He said he had lived next door once to a young lady who was learning to play the guitar, while a gentleman who practised on the bass viol lived opposite. And he, with fiendish cunning, had introduced these two unsuspecting young people to one another, and had persuaded them to elope with each other against their parents' wishes, and take their musical instruments with them; and they had done so, and, before the honeymoon was over, SHE had broken his head with the bass viol, and HE had tried to cram the guitar down her throat, and had injured her for life.

My friend said he used to lure muffin-men into the passage and then stuff them with their own wares till they burst and died. He said he had quieted eighteen that way.

Young men and women who recited long and dreary poems at evening parties, and callow youths who walked about the streets late at night, playing concertinas, he used to get together and poison in batches of ten, so as to save expense; and park orators and temperance lecturers he used to shut up six in a small room with a glass of water and a collection box apiece, and let them talk each other to death.

It did one good to listen to him.

I asked him when he expected the other ghosts – the ghosts of the wait and the cornet player, and the German band that Uncle John had mentioned. He smiled, and said they would never come again, any of them.

I said, 'Why, isn't it true, then, that they meet you here every Christmas Eve for a row?'

He replied that it WAS true. Every Christmas Eve, for twenty-five years, had he and they fought in that room; but they would never trouble him nor anybody else again. One by one, had he laid them out, spoilt, and utterly useless for all haunting purposes. He had finished off the last German-band ghost that very evening, just before I came upstairs, and had thrown what was left of it out through the slit between the window sashes. He said it would never be worth calling a ghost again.

'I suppose you will still come yourself, as usual?' I said. 'They would be sorry to miss you, I know.'

'Oh, I don't know,' he replied, 'there's nothing much to come for now. Unless,' he added kindly, 'YOU are going to be here. I'll come if you will sleep here next Christmas Eve.'

'I have taken a liking to you,' he continued, 'you don't fly off, screeching, when you see a party, and your hair doesn't stand on end. You've no idea,' he said, 'how sick I am of seeing people's hair standing on end.'

He said it irritated him.

Just then a slight noise reached us from the yard below, and he started and turned deathly black.

'You are ill,' I cried, springing towards him, 'tell me

the best thing to do for you. Shall I drink some brandy, and give you the ghost of it?'

He remained silent, listening intently for a moment, and then he gave a sigh of relief, and the shade came back to his cheek.

'It's all right,' he murmured, 'I was afraid it was the cock.'

'Oh, it's too early for that,' I said. 'Why, it's only the middle of the night.'

'Oh, that doesn't make any difference to those cursed chickens,' he replied bitterly. 'They would just as soon crow in the middle of the night as at any other time – sooner, if they thought it would spoil a chap's evening out. I believe they do it on purpose.'

He said a friend of his, the ghost of a man who had killed a water-rate collector, used to haunt a house in Long Acre, where they kept fowls in the cellar, and every time a policeman went by and flashed his bull'seye down the grating, the old cock there would fancy it was the sun, and start crowing like mad, when, of course, the poor ghost had to dissolve, and it would, in consequence, get back home sometimes as early as one o'clock in the morning, swearing fearfully because it had only been out for an hour.

I agreed that it seemed very unfair.

'Oh, it's an absurd arrangement altogether,' he

continued, quite angrily. 'I can't imagine what our old man could have been thinking of when he made it. As I have said to him, over and over again, "Have a fixed time, and let everybody stick to it – say four o'clock in summer, and six in winter. Then one would know what one was about."'

'How do you manage when there isn't any cock handy?' I inquired.

He was on the point of replying, when again he started and listened. This time I distinctly heard Mr Bowles's cock, next door, crow twice.

'There you are,' he said, rising and reaching for his hat, 'that's the sort of thing we have to put up with. What IS the time?'

I looked at my watch, and found it was half-past three.

'I thought as much,' he muttered. 'I'll wring that blessed bird's neck if I get hold of it.' And he prepared to go.

'If you can wait half a minute,' I said, getting out of bed, 'I'll go a bit of the way with you.'

'It's very good of you,' he rejoined, pausing, 'but it seems unkind to drag you out.'

'Not at all,' I replied, 'I shall like a walk.' And I partially dressed myself, and took my umbrella, and he put his arm through mine, and we went out together.

Just by the gate we met Jones, one of the local constables.

'Goodnight, Jones,' I said (I always feel affable at Christmas time).

'Goodnight, sir,' answered the man a little gruffly, I thought. 'May I ask what you're a-doing of?'

'Oh, it's all right,' I responded, with a wave of my umbrella, 'I'm just seeing my friend part of the way home.'

He said, 'What friend?'

'Oh, ah, of course,' I laughed. 'I forgot. He's invisible to you. He is the ghost of the gentleman that killed the wait. I'm just going to the corner with him.'

'Ah, I don't think I would, if I was you, sir,' said Jones severely. 'If you take my advice, you'll say goodbye to your friend here, and go back indoors. Perhaps you are not aware that you are walking about with nothing on but a nightshirt and a pair of boots and an opera hat. Where's your trousers?'

I did not like the man's manner at all. I said, 'Jones! I don't wish to have to report you, but it seems to me you've been drinking. My trousers are where a man's trousers ought to be – on his legs. I distinctly remember putting them on.'

'Well, you haven't got them on now,' he retorted.

'I beg your pardon,' I replied. 'I tell you I have; I think I ought to know.'

'I think so, too,' he answered, 'but you evidently don't.

Now you come along indoors with me, and don't let's have any more of it.'

Uncle John came to the door at this point, having been awaked, I suppose, by the altercation and, at the same moment, Aunt Maria appeared at the window in her nightcap.

I explained the constable's mistake to them, treating the matter as lightly as I could, so as not to get the man into trouble, and I turned for confirmation to the ghost.

He was gone! He had left me without a word – without even saying goodbye!

It struck me as so unkind, his having gone off in that way, that I burst into tears and Uncle John came out, and led me back into the house.

On reaching my room, I discovered that Jones was right. I had not put on my trousers, after all. They were still hanging over the bed rail. I suppose, in my anxiety not to keep the ghost waiting, I must have forgotten them.

Such are the plain facts of the case, out of which it must, doubtless, to the healthy, charitable mind appear impossible that calumny could spring.

But it has.

Persons – I say 'persons' – have professed themselves unable to understand the simple circumstances herein narrated, except in the light of explanations at once misleading and insulting. Slurs have been cast and aspersions made on me by those of my own flesh and blood.

But I bear no ill-feeling. I merely, as I have said, set forth this statement for the purpose of clearing my character from injurious suspicion.

The Lady and the Fox

KELLY LINK

Someone is in the garden.

'Daniel,' Miranda says. 'It's Santa Claus. He's looking in the window.'

'No, it's not,' Daniel says. He doesn't look. 'We've already had the presents. Besides. No such thing as Santa.'

They are together under the tree, the celebrated Honeywell Christmas tree.

They are both eleven years old. There's just enough space up against the trunk to sit cross-legged. Daniel is running the train set around the tree forwards, then backwards, then forwards again. Miranda is admiring her best present, a pair of gold-handled scissors shaped like a crane. The beak is the blade. Snip, snip, she slices brittle needles one by one off the branch above her. A smell of pine. A small green needle rain.

It must be very cold outside in the garden. The window shines with frost.

It's long past bedtime. If it isn't Santa Claus, it could be a burglar come to steal someone's jewels. Or an axe murderer.

Or else, of course, it's one of Daniel's hundreds of uncles or cousins.

Because there isn't a beard, and the face in the window isn't a jolly face.

Even partially obscured by darkness and frost, it has that Honeywell look to it. The room is full of adult Honeywells talking about the things that Honeywells always talk about, which is to say everything, horses and houses and God and grouting, tanning salons and – of course – theatre. Always theatre. Honeywells like to talk. When Honeywells have no lines to speak, they improvise. All the world's a stage.

Rare to see a Honeywell in isolation. They come bunched like bananas.

Not single spies, but in battalions. And as much as Miranda admires the red-gold Honeywell hair, the exaggerated, expressive Honeywell good looks, the Honeywell repertoire of jokes and confidences, poetry and nonsense, sometimes she needs an escape. Honeywells want you to talk, too. They ask questions until your mouth gets dry from answering.

Daniel is exceptionally restful for a Honeywell. He doesn't care if you are there or not.

Miranda wriggles out from under the tree, through the press of leggy Honeywells in black tie and party dresses: apocalyptically orange taffeta, slithering, clingy satins in canary and violet, foamy white silk already spotted with wine.

She is patted on the head, winked at. Someone in cloth of gold says, 'Poor little lamb.'

'Baaaah humbug,' Miranda blurts, beats on. Her own dress is green, finewale corduroy. Empire waist. Pinching at the armpits. Miranda's interest in these things is half professional. Her mother, Joannie (resident the last six months in a Phuket jail, will be there for many years to come), was Elspeth Honeywell's dresser and confidante.

Daniel is Elspeth's son. Miranda is Elspeth's goddaughter.

~

There are two men languorously kissing in the kitchen. Leaning against the sink, where one of the new Honeywell kittens licks sauce out of a gravy boat. A girl – only a few years older than Miranda – lays soiled and tattered Tarot cards out on the farmhouse table. Empty wine bottles tilt like cannons; a butcher knife sheathed in a demolished Christmas cake. Warmth seeps from the stove:

just inside the Aga's warming drawer, Miranda can see the other kittens, asleep in a crusted pan.

Miranda picks up a bag of party trash, lipstick-blotted napkins, throwaway champagne glasses, greasy fragments of pastry, hauls it out through the kitchen door. Mama cat slips inside as Miranda goes out.

Snow is falling. Big, sticky clumps that melt on her hair, her cheeks. Snow on Christmas. None in Phuket, of course. She wonders what they give you to eat on Christmas Day in a Thai prison. Her mother always makes the Christmas cake. Miranda helps roll out the marzipan in sheets. Her ballet flats skid on the grass.

She ties the bag, leaves it against the steps. And here is the man in the garden, still standing before the window, looking in.

He must hear Miranda. Surely he hears her. Her feet upon the frozen grass. But he doesn't turn around.

Even seen from the back, he is recognizably a Honeywell. Lanky, yellow-haired; perfectly still, he is somehow perfectly still, perfectly posed to catch the eye. Unnaturally natural. The snow that is making Miranda's nose run, her cheeks blotchy with cold, rests unmelted upon the bright Honeywell hair, the shoulders of the surprising coat.

Typical Honeywell behaviour, Miranda thinks. A lovers' quarrel, or else he's taken offense at something someone said, and is now going to sulk himself hand-somely to death in the cold. Her mother has been quite clear about how to behave when a Honeywell is being dramatic when drama isn't required. Firmness is the key.

At this last thought of her mother, Miranda has some dramatic feelings of her own. She focuses on the coat, sends the feelings away. It is quite a coat. A costume? Pilfered from some production. Eighteenth century. Beautifully cut. Not a frock coat. A *justacorps*. Rose damask. Embroidered all over with white silk thread, poppies and roses, and there, where it flares out over the hips, a staghorn beetle on a green leaf. She has come nearer and nearer, cannot stop herself from reaching out to touch the beetle.

She almost expects her hand to pass right through. (Surely there are ghosts at Honeywell Hall.) But it doesn't. The coat is real. Miranda pinches the damask between her fingers. Says, 'Whatever it is that happened, it isn't worth freezing to death over. You shouldn't be out here. You should come inside.'

The Honeywell in the *justacorps* turns around then. 'I am exactly where I am supposed to be,' he says. 'Which is here. Doing precisely what I am supposed to be doing. Which does not include having conversations with little girls. Go away, little girl.'

Little girl she may be, but Miranda is well armored

already against the Honeywell arsenal of tantrums, tempests, ups, downs, charm, strange.

Above the wide right pocket of the *justacorps* is a fox stitched in red and gold, its foreleg caught in a trap.

'I'm Miranda,' she says. And then, because she's picked up a Honeywell trick or two herself, she says, 'My mother's in jail.'

The Honeywell looks almost sympathetic for the briefest of moments, then shrugs. Theatrically, of course. Sticks his hands in his pockets. 'What's that got to do with me?'

'Everyone's got problems, that's all,' Miranda says. 'I'm here because Elspeth feels sorry for me. I hate when people feel sorry for me. And I don't feel sorry for you. I don't know you. I just don't think it's very smart, standing out here because you're in a mood. But maybe you aren't very smart. My mother says good-looking people often don't bother. What's your name?'

'If I tell you, will you go away?' the Honeywell says.

'Yes,' Miranda says. She can go in the kitchen and play with the kittens. Do the dishes and be useful. Have her fortune told. Sit under the tree again with Daniel until it's well past time to go to sleep. Tomorrow she'll be sent away home on a bus. By next year Elspeth will have most likely forgotten she has a goddaughter.

'I'm Fenny,' the Honeywell says. 'Now go away. I have

things to not do, and not a lot of time to not do them in.'

'Well,' Miranda says. She pats Fenny on the broad cuff of the sleeve of his lovely coat. She wonders what the lining is. How cold he must be. How stupid he is, standing out here when he is welcome inside. 'Merry Christmas. Goodnight.'

She reaches out one last time, touches the embroidered fox, its leg caught in the trap. Stem stitch and seed stitch and herringbone. 'It's very fine work, truly,' she says. 'But I hope he gets free.'

'He was stupid to get caught,' Fenny says, 'you peculiar and annoying child.' He is already turning back to the window. What does he see through it? When Miranda is finally back inside the drawing room where tipsy Honeywells are all roaring out inappropriate lyrics to carols, pulling Christmas crackers, putting on paper crowns, she looks through the window. The snow has stopped. No one is there.

~

But Elspeth Honeywell, as it happens, remembers Miranda the next year and the year and the year after that. There are presents for Miranda under the magnificent tree. A ticket to a London musical that she never sees. A make-up kit when she is thirteen.

The year she is eleven, Daniel gives her a chess set and a box of assorted skeins of silk thread. Under her black tights, Miranda wears a red braided leather anklet that came in an envelope, no letter, from Phuket. The kittens are all grown up and pretend not to know her.

The year she is twelve, she looks for the mysterious Fenny. He isn't there. When she asks, no one knows who she means.

The year she is thirteen, she has champagne for the first time.

The Christmas she is fourteen, she feels quite grown up. The man in the *justacorps* was a dream, or some story she made up for herself in order to feel interesting. At fourteen she's outgrown fairytales, Santa Claus, ghost stories. When Daniel points out that they are standing under the mistletoe, she kisses him once on each cheek. And then sticks her tongue in his ear.

~

It snows again the Christmas she is fifteen. Snow is predicted, snow falls. Something about the chance of snow makes her think of him again. The man in the snowy garden. There is no man in the garden, of course; there never was. But there is Honeywell Hall, which is enough – and seemingly endless heaps of Honeywell adults behaving as if they were children again.

It's exhausting, almost Olympic, the amount of fun Honeywells seem to require. She can't decide if it's awful or if it's wonderful.

Late in the afternoon the Honeywells are playing charades. No fun, playing with people who do this professionally. Miranda stands at the window, watching the snow fall, looking for something. Birds. A fox. A man in the garden.

A Honeywell shouts, 'Good god, no! Cleopatra came rolled up in a carpet, not in the Sunday supplement!'

Daniel is up in his room, talking to his father on Skype.

Miranda moves from window to window, pretending she is not looking for anything in particular. Far down the grounds, she sees something out of place. Someone. She's out the door in a flash.

'Going for a walk!' she yells while the door is swinging closed. In case anyone cares.

She finds the man navigating along the top of the old perimeter wall, stepping stone to stone. Fenny. He knocks a stick against each stone as he goes.

'You,' he says. 'I wondered if I'd see you again.'

'Miranda,' she says. 'I bet you forgot.'

'No,' he says. 'I didn't. Want to come up?'

He holds out his hand. She hesitates, and he says, 'Suit yourself.'

'I can get up by myself,' she says, and does. She's in front of him now. Walks backwards so that she can keep an eye on him.

'You're not a Honeywell,' he says.

'No,' she says. 'You are.'

'Yes,' he says. 'Sort of.'

She stops then, so that he has to stop, too. It isn't like they could keep on going anyway. There's a gap in the wall just behind her.

'I remember when they built this wall,' he says.

She's probably misheard him. Or else he's teasing her. She says, 'You must be very old.'

'Older than you anyway,' he says. He sits down on the wall, so she sits down, too. Honeywell Hall is in front of them. There's a copse of woods behind. Snow falls lazily, a bit of wind swirling it, tossing it up again.

'Why do you always wear that coat?' Miranda says. She fidgets a little. Her bum is getting cold. 'You shouldn't sit on a dirty wall. It's too nice.' She touches the embroidered beetle, the fox.

'Someone very . . . special gave it to me,' he says. 'I wear it always because it is her wish that I do so.' The way he says it makes Miranda shiver just a little.

'Right,' she says. 'Like my anklet. My mother sent it to me. She's in prison. She'll never get out. She'll be there until she dies.'

'Like the fox,' he says.

'Like your fox,' Miranda says. She's horrified to find that her eyes are watering. Is she crying? It isn't even a real fox. She doesn't want to look at the man in the coat, Fenny, to see if he's noticed, so she jumps down off the wall and begins to walk back toward the house.

When she's halfway to the Hall, the drifting snow stops. She looks back; no one sits on the wall.

~

The snow stops and starts, on and off all day long. When dinner is finished, Honeywells groaning, clutching their bellies, Elspeth has something for Miranda. Elspeth says, wagging the present between two fingers like it's a special treat, and Miranda some stray puppy. 'Someone left it on the doorstep for you, Miranda. I wonder who.'

The wrapping is a sheet of plain white stationery, tied with a bit of green thread. Her name in a scratchy hand. *Miranda.* Inside is a scrap of rose damask, the embroidered fox, snarling; the mangled leg, the bloodied trap.

'Let me see, sweet,' Elspeth says, and takes the rose damask from her. 'What a strange present! A joke?'

'I don't know,' Miranda says. 'Maybe.'

It's eight o'clock. Honeywell Hall, up on its hill, must shine like a torch. Miranda puts on her coat and walks around the house three times. The snow has all melted.

Daniel intercepts her on the final circuit. He's pimply, knobbly at present, and his nose is too big for his face. She loves him dearly, just like she loves Elspeth. They are always kind to her. 'Here,' he says, handing her the bit of damask. 'Secret Santa? Secret admirer? Secret code?'

'Oh, you know,' Miranda says. 'Long story. Saving it for my memoirs.'

'Meanwhile back in there everyone's pretending it's 1970 and they're all sweet sixteen again. Playing Sardines and drinking. It'll be orgies in all the cupboards, dramatic confessions and attempted murders in the pantry, under the stairs, in the beds and under them all night long. So I took this and snuck out.' Daniel shows her the bottle of Strongbow in his coat pocket. 'Let's go and sit in the Tiger. You can tell me all about school and the agony aunt, I'll tell you which Tory MP Elspeth's been seeing on the sly. Then you can sell the story to the *Sun*.'

'And use the proceeds to buy us a cold-water flat in Wolverhampton. We'll live the life,' Miranda says.

They drink the cider and eat a half-melted Mars bar. They talk and Miranda wonders if Daniel will try to kiss her. If she should try to kiss Daniel. But he doesn't, she doesn't – they don't – and she falls asleep on the mouse-eaten upholstery of the preposterous carcass of the Sunbeam Tiger, her head on Daniel's shoulder, the trapped fox crumpled in her fist.

Christmas after, Elspeth is in all the papers. The Tory MP's husband is divorcing her. Elspeth is a co-respondent in the divorce. Meanwhile she has a new thing with a footballer twenty years her junior. It's the best kind of Christmas story. Journalists everywhere. Elspeth, in the Sunbeam Tiger, picks up Miranda at the station in a wide-brimmed black hat, black jumpsuit, black sunglasses, triumphantly disgraced. In her element.

Miranda's aunt almost didn't let her come this year. But then, if Miranda had stayed, they would have both been miserable. Her aunt has a new boyfriend. Almost as awful as she is. Someone should tell the tabloids.

'Lovely dress,' Elspeth says, kissing her on the cheek. 'You make it?' Miranda is particularly pleased with the hem.

'It's all right.'

'I want one just like it,' Elspeth says. 'In red. Lower the neckline, raise the hem a bit. You could go into business. Ever think of it?'

'I'm only sixteen,' Miranda says. 'There's plenty of room for improvement.'

'Alexander McQueen! Left school when he was sixteen,' Elspeth says.

'Went off to apprentice on Savile Row. Used to sew human hair into his linings. A kind of spell, I suppose. I have one of his manta dresses somewhere in the Hall.

And your mother, she was barely older than you are now. Hanging around backstage, stitching sequins and crystals on tulle.'

'Where's Daniel?' Miranda says. She and her mother have been corresponding. Miranda is saving up money. She hasn't told her aunt yet, but next summer Miranda's going to Thailand.

'Back at the house. In a mood. Listening to my old records. The Smiths.' Miranda looks over, studies Elspeth's face. 'That girl broke up with him, didn't she?'

'If you mean the one with the ferrets and the unfortunate ankles,' Elspeth says, 'yes. What's her name. It's a mystery. Not her name, the breakup. He grows three inches in two months, his skin clears up, honestly, Miranda, he's even better looking than I expected he'd turn out. Heart of gold, that boy, a good brain, too. I can't think what she was thinking.'

'Preemptive strike, perhaps,' Miranda says.

'I wouldn't know about the breakup except for accidentally overhearing a conversation. Somewhat accidentally,' Elspeth says. 'Well, that and the Smiths. He doesn't talk to me about his love life.'

'Do you *want* him to talk to you about his love life?'

'No,' Elspeth says. 'Yes. Maybe? Probably not. Anyway,

how about you, Miranda? Do you have one of those, yet? A love life?'

'I don't even have ferrets,' Miranda says.

~

On Christmas Eve, while all the visiting Honeywells and cousins and wives and boyfriends and girlfriends and their accountants are out caroling in the village, Elspeth takes Miranda and Daniel aside. She gives them each a joint.

'It's not as if I don't know you've been raiding my supply, Daniel,' Elspeth says. 'At least this way, I know what you're up to. If you're going to break the law, you might as well learn to break it responsibly. Under adult supervision.'

Daniel rolls his eyes, looks at Miranda. Whatever he sees in her face makes him snort. It's annoying but true: he really has become quite spectacular looking. Well, it was inevitable. Apparently they drown all the ugly Honeywells at birth.

'It's okay, Mi*randy*,' he says. 'I'll have yours if you don't want it.' Miranda sticks the joint in her bra. 'Thanks, but I'll hang on to it.'

'Anyway I'm sure the two of you have lots of catching up to do,' Elspeth says. 'I'm off to the pub to kiss the barmaids and make the journos cry.'

When she's out the door, Daniel says, 'She's match-making, isn't she?'

Miranda says, 'Or else it's reverse psychology?'

Their eyes meet. *Courage, Miranda.* Daniel tilts his head, looks gleeful. 'In which case, I should do this,' he says. He leans forward, puts his hand on Miranda's chin, tilts it up. 'We should do this.'

He kisses her. His lips are soft and dry. Miranda sucks on the bottom one experimentally. She arranges her arms around his neck, and his hands go down, cup her bum. He opens his mouth and does things with his tongue until she opens her mouth, too. He seems to know how this goes; he and the girl with the ferrets probably did this a lot.

Miranda wonders if the ferrets were in the cage at the time, or out. How unsettling is it, she wonders, to fool around with ferrets watching you? Their beady button eyes.

She can feel Daniel's erection. Oh, God. How embarrassing. She pushes him away. 'Sorry,' she groans. 'Sorry! Yeah, no, I don't think we should be doing this. Any of this!'

'Probably not,' Daniel says. 'Probably definitely not. It's weird, right?'

'It's weird,' Miranda says.

'But perhaps it wouldn't be so weird if we smoked a joint first,' Daniel says. His hair is messy. Apparently she did that.

'Or,' Miranda says, 'maybe we could just smoke a joint. And, you know, not complicate things.'

Halfway through the joint, Daniel says, 'It wouldn't

have to complicate everything.' His head is in her lap. She's curling pieces of his hair around her finger.

'Yes, it would,' Miranda says. 'It *really, really* would.'

Later on she says, 'I wish it would snow. That would be nice. If it snowed. I thought that's why you lot came here at Christmas. The whole white Christmas thing.'

'Awful stuff,' Daniel says. 'Cold. Slippy. Makes you feel like you're supposed to be singing or something. In a movie. Or in a snow globe.'

'Stuck,' Miranda says. 'Trapped.'

'Stuck,' Daniel says.

They're lying, tangled together, on a sofa across from the Christmas tree.

Occasionally Miranda has to remove Daniel's hand from somewhere it shouldn't be. She doesn't think he's doing it intentionally. She kisses him behind the ear now and then. 'That's nice,' he says. Pats her bum. She wriggles out from under his hand. Kisses him again. There's a movie on television, lots of explosions. Zombies. Cameron Diaz unloading groceries in a cottage, all by herself.

No, that's another movie entirely, Miranda thinks. Apparently she's been asleep. Daniel is still sleeping. Why does he have to be so irritatingly good looking, even in his sleep? Miranda hates to think what she looks like asleep.

No wonder the ferret girl dumped him.

Elspeth must have come back from the pub, because there's a heap of blankets over the both of them.

Outside, it's snowing.

Miranda puts her hand in the pocket of her dress, feels the piece of damask she has had there all day long. It's a big pocket. Plenty of room for all kinds of things. Miranda doesn't want to be one of those designers who only makes pretty things. She wants them to be useful, too. And provoking. She takes the prettiest blanket from the sofa for herself, distributes the other blankets over Daniel so that all of him is covered.

She goes by a mirror, stops to smooth her hair down, collect it into a ponytail.

Wraps the blanket around herself like a shawl, goes out into the snow. He's there, under the hawthorn tree. She shivers, tells herself it's because of the cold. There isn't much snow on the ground yet. She tells herself she hasn't been asleep too long. He hasn't been waiting long.

He wears the same coat. His face is the same. He isn't as old as she thought he was, that first time. Only a few years older than she. Than Daniel. He hasn't aged. She has. Where is he, when he isn't here?

'Are you a ghost?' she says.

'No,' he says. 'I'm not a ghost.'

'Then you're a real person? A Honeywell?'

'Fenwick Septimus Honeywell.' He bows. It looks

better than it should, probably because of the coat. People don't really do that sort of thing anymore. No one has names like that. How old is he?

'You only come when it snows,' she says.

'I am only allowed to come when it's snowing,' he says. 'And only on Christmas Day.'

'Right,' she says. 'Okay, no. No, I don't understand. Allowed by whom?' He shrugs. Doesn't answer. Maybe it isn't allowed.

'You gave me something,' Miranda says.

He nods again. She puts out her hand, touches the place on the *justacorps* where he tore away the fox. So he could give it to her.

'Oh,' Miranda said. 'The poor old thing. You didn't even use scissors, did you? Let me fix it.'

She takes the piece of damask out of her pocket, along with her sewing kit, the one she always keeps with her. She's had exactly the right thread in there for over a year. Just in case.

She shows him the damask. A few months ago she unpicked all of the fox's leg, all of the trap. The drops of blood. The tail and snarling head. Then she reworked the embroidery to her own design, mimicking as closely as possible the feel of the original. Now the fox is free, tongue lolling, tail aloft, running along the pink plane of the damask. Pink cotton backing, a piece she cut from an old nightgown.

He takes it from her, turns it over in his hand. 'You did this?'

'You gave me a present last year. This is my present for you,' she says.

'I'll sew it back in. It will be a little untidy, but at least you won't have a hole in your lovely coat.'

He says, 'I told her I tore it on a branch. It's fine just as it is.'

'It isn't fine,' she says. 'Let me fix it, please.'

He smiles. It's a real smile, maybe even a flirtatious smile. He and Daniel could be brothers. They're that much alike. So why did she stop Daniel from kissing her? Why does she have to bite her tongue, sometimes, when Daniel is being kind to her? At Honeywell Hall, she is only as real as Elspeth and Daniel allow her to be. This isn't her real life.

It's ridiculous, of course. Real is real. Daniel is real. Miranda is real when she isn't here. Whatever Fenwick Septimus Honeywell is, Miranda's fairly sure it's complicated.

'*Please,*' she says.

'As you wish it, Miranda,' Fenny says. She helps him out of the coat. Her hand touches his, and she pushes down the inexplicable desire to clutch at it.

As if one of them were falling.

'Come inside the Hall,' she says. 'Just while I'm working on this. I should do it inside. Better light. You could meet

Daniel. Or Elspeth. I could wake her up. I bet Elspeth knows how to deal with this sort of thing.' Whatever this sort of thing is. 'Theatre people seem like they know how to deal with things like this. Come inside with me.'

'I can't,' he says regretfully.

Of course. It's against the rules.

'Okay,' Miranda says, adjusting. 'Then we'll both stay out here. I'll stay with you. You can tell me all about yourself. Unless that's against the rules too.' She busies herself with pins. He lifts her hand away, holds it. 'Inside out, if you please,' he says. 'The fox on the inside.' He has lovely hands. No calluses on his fingertips. Manicured nails.

Definitely not real. His thumb smooths over her knuckles. Miranda says, a little breathless, 'Inside out. So she won't notice someone's repaired it?'

Whoever *she* is.

'She'll notice,' he says. 'But this way she won't see that the fox is free.'

'Okay. That's sensible. I guess.' Miranda lets go of his hand. 'Here. We can sit on this.'

She spreads out the blanket. Sits down. Remembers she has a Mars bar in her pocket. She passes that to him. 'Sit.'

He examines the Mars bar. Unwraps it.

'Oh, no,' she says. 'More rules? You're not allowed to eat?'

'I don't know,' he says. 'I've never been given anything before. When I came. No one has ever talked to me.'

'So you show up when it snows, creep around for a while, looking in at the windows. Then you go back wherever when the snow stops.' Fenny nods. He looks almost abashed.

'What fun!' Miranda says. 'Wait, no, I mean how creepy!' She has the piece of embroidery how she wants it, is tacking it into place with running stitches, so the fox is hidden.

If it stops snowing, will he just disappear? Will the coat stay? Something tells her that all of this is very against the rules. Does he want to come back?

And what does she mean by *back*, anyway? Back here, to Honeywell Hall?

Or back to wherever it is that he is when he isn't here? Why doesn't he get older?

Elspeth says it's a laugh, getting older. But oh, Miranda knows, Elspeth doesn't mean it.

'It's good,' Fenny says, sounding surprised. The Mars bar is gone. He's licking his fingers.

'I could go back in the house,' Miranda says. 'I could make you a cheese sandwich. There's Christmas cake for tomorrow.'

'No,' he says. 'Stay.'

'Okay,' she says. 'I'll stay. Here. That's the best I can do in this light. My hands are getting too cold.'

He takes the coat from her. Nods. Then puts it around

her shoulders. Pulls her back against his chest. All of that damask: it's heavy. There's snow inside and out.

Fenny is surprisingly solid for someone who mostly isn't here. She wonders if she is surprising to him, too.

His mouth is just above the top of her head, blowing little hot circles against her hair. She's very, very cold. Ridiculous to be out here in the snow with this ridiculous person with his list of ridiculous rules.

She'll catch her death of cold.

Cautiously, as if he's waiting for her to stop him, he puts his arms around her waist. He sighs. Warm breath in her hair. Miranda is suddenly so very afraid that it will stop snowing. They haven't talked about anything. They haven't even kissed. She knows, every part of her knows, that she wants to kiss him. That he wants to kiss her. All of her skin prickles with longing. Her insides fizz.

She puts her sewing kit back into her pocket, discovers the joint Elspeth gave her, Daniel's lighter. 'I bet you haven't ever tried this, either,' she says.

She twists in his arms. 'You smoke it. Here.' She taps at the side of his face with the joint, sticks it between his lips when they part. Flicks the lighter until it catches, and then she's lunging at him, kissing him, and he's kissing her back. The second time tonight that she's kissed a boy, the first two boys she's ever kissed, and both of them Honeywells.

And oh, it was lovely kissing Daniel, but this is something better than lovely. All they do is kiss, she doesn't know how long they kiss; at first Fenny tastes of chocolate, and she doesn't know what happens to the joint. Or to the lighter. They kiss until Miranda's lips are numbish and the *justacorps* has come entirely off of her, and she's in Fenny's lap and she has one hand in Fenny's hair and one hand digging into Fenny's waist, and all she wants to do is keep on kissing Fenny forever and ever. Until he pulls away. They're both breathing hard. His cheeks are red. His mouth is redder.

Miranda wonders if she looks as crazed as he looks.

'You're shivering,' he says.

'Of course I'm shivering! It's freezing out here! And you won't come inside. Because,' Miranda says, panting, shivering, all of her vibrating with cold and with want, want, want, 'it's against the rules!'

Fenny nods. Looks at her lips, licks his own. Jerks back, though, when Miranda tries to kiss him again. She's tempted to pick up a handful of wet snow and smush it into his Honeywell face.

'Fine, fine! You stay right here. Don't move. Not even an inch, understand? I'll get the keys to the Tiger,' she says. 'Unless it's against the rules to sit in old cars.'

'All of this is against the rules,' Fenny says. But he nods. Maybe, she thinks, she can get him in the car and just drive away with him. Maybe that would work.

'I mean it,' Miranda says. 'Don't you dare go anywhere.'

He nods. She kisses him, punishingly, lingeringly, desperately, then takes off in a run for the kitchen. Her fingers are so cold she can't get the door open at first. She grabs her coat, the keys to the Tiger, and then, on impulse, cuts off a hunk of the inviolate Christmas cake. Well, if Elspeth says anything, she'll tell her the whole story.

Then she's out the door again. Says the worst words she knows when she sees that the snow has stopped. There is the snow-blotted blanket, the joint, and the Mars bar wrapper.

She leaves the Christmas cake on the window ledge. Maybe the birds will eat it.

~

Daniel is still asleep on the couch. She wakes him up. 'Merry Christmas,' she says. 'Good morning.' She gives him his present. She's made him a shirt. Egyptian cotton, gray-blue to match his eyes. But of course it won't fit. He's already outgrown it.

~

Daniel catches her under the mistletoe when it's past time for bed, Christmas night and no one wants to go to sleep yet, everyone tipsy and loose and picking fights about things they don't care about. For the sheer pleasure of picking fights. He kisses Miranda. She lets him.

It's sort of a present for Elspeth, Miranda rationalizes. It's sort of because she knows it's ridiculous, not kissing Daniel, just because she wants to be kissing someone else instead. Especially when the person she wants to be kissing isn't really a real person at all. At least not most of the time.

Besides, he's wearing the shirt Miranda made for him, even though it doesn't fit.

In the morning, Daniel is too hung over to drive her down to the village to catch the bus. Elspeth takes her instead. Elspeth is wearing a vintage suit, puce gabardine, trimmed with sable, something Miranda itches to take apart, just to see how it's made. What a tiny waist she has.

Elspeth says, 'You know he's in love with you.'

'He's not,' Miranda says. 'He loves me, but he's not in love with me. I love him, but I'm not in love with him.'

'If you say so,' Elspeth says. Her tone is cool. 'Although I can't help being curious how you've come to know so much about love, Miranda, at your tender age.'

Miranda flushes.

'You know you can talk to me,' Elspeth says. 'You can

talk to me whenever you want to. Whenever you need to. Darling Miranda. There's a boy, isn't there? Not Daniel. Poor Daniel.'

'There's nobody,' Miranda says. 'Really. There's nobody. It's nothing. I'm just a bit sad because I have to go home again. It was such a lovely Christmas.'

'Such lovely snow!' Elspeth says. 'Too bad it never lasts.'

~

Daniel comes to visit in the spring. Two months after Christmas. Miranda isn't expecting him. He shows up at the door with a bouquet of roses. Miranda's aunt's eyebrows go almost up to her hairline. 'I'll make tea,' she says, and scurries off. 'And we'll need a vase for those.'

Miranda takes the roses from Daniel. Says, 'Daniel! What are you doing here?'

'You've been avoiding me,' Daniel says.

'Avoiding you? We don't live in the same place,' Miranda says. 'I wasn't even sure you knew where I lived.' She can hardly stand to have him here, standing in the spotless foyer of her aunt's semidetached bungalow.

'You know what I mean, Miranda. You're never online,' he says. 'And when you are, you never want to chat. You never text me back. Aren't you going to invite me in?'

'No,' she says. Grabs her bag.

'Don't bother with the tea, Aunt Dora,' she says loudly, 'We're going out.'

She yanks at Daniel's hand, extracts him violently from her life, her *real* life. If only.

She speed walks him past the tract houses with their small, white-stone frontages, all the way to the dreary, dingy, Midlands-typical High Street. Daniel trailing behind her. It's a long walk, and she has no idea what to say to him. He doesn't seem to know what to say, either.

Her dress is experimental, nothing she's ever intended to wear out. She hasn't yet brushed her hair today. It's the weekend. She was planning to stay in and study. How dare he show up.

There's a teashop where the scones and the sandwiches are particularly foul. She takes him there, and they sit down. Order.

'I should have let you know I was coming,' Daniel says.

'Yes,' Miranda says. 'Then I could have told you not to.'

He tries to take her hand. 'Mirandy,' he says. 'I think about you all the time. About us. I think about us.'

'Don't,' she says. 'Stop!'

'I can't,' he says. 'I like you. Very much. Don't you like me?'

It's a horrible conversation. Like stepping on a baby mouse. A baby mouse who happens to be your friend. It doesn't help that Miranda knows how unfair she's being. She shouldn't be angry that he's come here. He doesn't know how she feels about this place. Just a few more months and she'll be gone from here forever. It will never have existed.

They are both practically on the verge of tears by the time the scones come. Daniel takes one bite and then spits it out onto the plate.

'It's not that bad,' she snaps. Dares him to complain.

'Yes it is,' he says. 'It really truly is that bad.' He takes a sip of his tea. 'And the milk has gone off, too.'

He seems so astonished at this that she can't help it. She bursts out laughing. This astonishes him, too. And just like that, they aren't fighting anymore. They spend the rest of the day feeding ducks at the frozen pond, going in and out of horror movies, action movies, cartoons – all the movies except the romantic comedies, because why rub salt in the wound? – at the cinema. He doesn't try to hold her hand. She tries not to imagine that it is snowing outside, that it is Fenny sitting in the flickering darkness here beside her. Imagining this is against the rules.

~

Miranda finishes out the term. Packs up what she wants to take with her, boxes up the rest. Sells her sewing machine. Leaves a note for her aunt. Never mind what's in it.

She knows she should be more grateful. Her aunt has kept her fed, kept her clothed, given her bed and board. Never hit her. Never, really, been unkind. But Miranda is so very, very tired of being grateful to people.

She is sticky, smelly, and punch-drunk with jetlag when her flight arrives in Phuket. Stays the night in a hostel and then sets off. She's read about how this is supposed to go. What you can bring, how long you can stay, how you should behave. All the rules.

But, in the end, she doesn't see Joannie. It isn't allowed. It isn't clear why. Is her mother there? They tell her yes. Is she still alive? Yes. Can Miranda see her? No. Not possible today. Come back.

Miranda comes back three times. Each time she is sent away. The consul can't help. On her second visit, she speaks to a young woman named Dinda, who comes and spends time with the prisoners when they are in the infirmary. Dinda says that she's sat with Joannie two or three times. That Miranda's mother never says much.

It's been over six months since her mother wrote to either Elspeth or to Miranda.

The third time she is sent away, Miranda buys a plane ticket to Japan. She spends the next four months there, teaching English in Kyoto. Going to museums. Looking at kimonos at the flea markets at the temples.

She sends postcards to Elspeth, to Daniel. To her mother. She even sends one to her aunt. And two days before Christmas, Miranda flies home.

On the plane, she falls asleep and dreams that it's snowing. She's with Joannie in a cell in the prison in Phuket. Her mother tells Miranda that she loves her. She tells her that her sentence has been commuted. She tells her that if Miranda's good and follows the rules very carefully, she'll be home by Christmas.

～

She has a plan this year. The plan is that it will snow on Christmas. Never mind what the forecast says. It will snow. She will find Fenny. And she won't leave his side. Never mind what the rules say.

Daniel is going to St. Andrews next year. His girlfriend's name is Lillian. Elspeth is on her best behavior. Miranda is, too. She tells various Honeywells amusing stories about her students, the deer at the temples, and the girl who played the flute for them.

Elspeth is getting *old*. She's still the most beautiful woman Miranda has ever seen, but she's in her sixties now. Any day she'll be given a knighthood and never be scandalous again.

Lillian is a nice person. She tells Miranda that she likes Miranda's dress. She flirts with the most decrepit of the Honeywells, helps set the table. Daniel watches everything that she does as if all of it is brand new, as if Lillian has invented compliments, flirting, as if there were no such thing as water glasses and table linens before Lillian discovered them. Oh newfound land.

Despite all this, Miranda thinks she could be fond of Lillian. She's smart. Likes maths. Actually, truly, *really* seems to like Miranda's dress, which, let's admit it, is meant as an act of war. Miranda is not into pretty at the moment. She's into armor, weaponry, abrasiveness, discomfort – hers and other peoples'. The dress is leather, punk, studded with spikes, buckles, metal cuffs, chain looped round and around. Whenever she sits down, she has to be careful not to gash, impale, or skewer the furniture. Hugging is completely out of the question.

～

Lillian wants a tour, so after dinner and the first round of cocktails, Miranda and Daniel take her all through Honeywell Hall, the parts that are kept up and the parts that are falling into shadow. They end up in one of the attics, digging through Elspeth's trunks of costumes. They make Lillian try on cheesecloth dresses, hand-beaded fairy wings, ancient, cakey stage make-up. Take selfies. Daniel reads old mail from fans, pulls out old photos of Elspeth and Joannie, backstage. Here's Joannie perched on a giant urn. Joannie, her mouth full of pins. Joannie, at a first-night party, drunk and laughing and young. It should hurt to look at these pictures. Shouldn't it?

'Do you think it will snow?' Lillian says. 'I want snow for Christmas.'

Daniel says, 'Snowed last Christmas. Shouldn't expect that it will, this year. Too warm.'

Not even trying to sound casual about it, Miranda says, 'It's going to snow. It has to snow. And if it doesn't snow, then we're going to do something about it. We'll make it snow.'

She feels quite gratified when Lillian looks at her as if Miranda is insane, possibly dangerous. Well, the dress should have told her that.

'My present this year,' Miranda says, 'is going to be snow. Call me the Snow Queen. Come and see.'

Her suitcases – her special equipment – barely fit into the Tiger. Elspeth didn't say a word, just raised an eyebrow. Most of it is still in the carriage house.

Daniel is game when she explains. Lillian is either game, or pretending to be. There are long, gauzy swathes of white cloth to weave through tree branches, to tack down to the ground. There are long strings of glass and crystal and silver ornaments. Hand-cut lace snowflakes caught in netting. The pièce de résistance is the Snowboy Stage Whisper Fake Snow Machine with its fifty-foot extending hose reel. Miranda's got bags and bags of fake snow. Over an hour's worth of the best quality fake snow money can buy, according to the guy who rented her the Snowboy.

It's nearly midnight by the time they have everything arranged to Miranda's satisfaction. She goes inside and turns on the Hall's floodlights, then turns on the snow machine. A fine, glittering snow begins. Lillian kisses Daniel lingeringly. A fine romance.

Elspeth has been observing the whole time from the kitchen stair. She puts a hand over her cocktail. Fake snow dusts her fair hair, streaks it white.

All of the Honeywells who haven't gone to bed yet, which is most of them, *ooh* and *ah*. The youngest Honeywells, the ones who weren't even born when Miranda first came to Honeywell Hall, break into a spontaneous round of applause. Miranda feels quite powerful. Santa Claus exists after all.

~

All of the Honeywells eventually retreat into the house to drink and gossip and admire Miranda's special effects from within. It may not be properly cold tonight, but it's cold enough. Time for hot chocolate, hot toddies, hot baths, hot water bottles and bed.

She's not sure, of course, that this will work. If this is playing by the rules. But isn't she owed something by now? A bit of luck?

And she is. At first, not daring to hope, she thinks that Daniel has come from the Hall to fetch her in. But it isn't Daniel.

Fenny, in that old *justacorps*, Miranda's stitching around the piece above his pocket, walks out from under the hawthorn tree.

'It worked,' Miranda says. She hugs herself, which is a mistake. All those spikes. 'Ow. Oh.'

'I shouldn't be here, should I?' Fenny says. 'You've done something.' Miranda looks closely at his face. How young he looks. Barely older than she. How long has he been this young?

Fake snow is falling on their heads. 'We have about an hour,' Miranda says. 'Not much time.'

He comes to her then, takes her in his arms. 'Be careful,' she says. 'I'm all spikes.'

'A ridiculous dress,' he says into her hair. 'Though comely. Is this what people wear in this age?'

'Says the man wearing a *justacorps*,' she says. They're almost the same height this year. He's shorter than Daniel now, she realizes. Then they're kissing, she and Fenny are kissing, and she isn't thinking about Daniel at all.

They kiss, and Fenny presses himself against her, armored with spikes though Miranda is. He holds her, hands just above her waist, tight enough that she thinks she will have bruises in the shape of his fingers.

'Come in the Hall with me,' Miranda says, in between kisses. 'Come with me.'

Fenny bites her lower lip. Then licks it. 'Can't,' he says.

'Because of the rules.' Now he's nibbling her ear. She whimpers. Tugs him away by the hair. 'Hateful rules.'

'Could I stay with you, I vow I would. I would stay and grow old with you, Miranda. Or as long as you wanted me to stay.'

'Stay with me,' she says. Her dress must be goring into him. His stomach, his thighs. They'll both be black and blue tomorrow.

He doesn't say anything. Kisses her over and over. Distracting her, she knows. The front of her dress fastens with a simple clasp. Underneath she's wearing an old T-shirt. Leggings. She guides his hands.

'If you can't stay with me,' she says, as Fenny opens the clasp, 'then I'll stay with you.'

His hands are on her rib cage as she speaks. Simple enough to draw him inside the armature of the dress, to reach behind his back, pull the belt of heavy chain around them both. Fasten it. The key is in the Hall. In the attic, where she left it.

'Miranda,' Fenny says, when he realizes. 'What have you done?'

'A crucial component of any relationship is the capacity to surprise the one you love. I read that somewhere. A magazine. You're going to love women's magazines. Oh, and the Internet. Well, parts of it anyway. I won't let you go,' Miranda says. The dress is a snug fit for two people. She can feel every breath he takes. 'If you go, then I'll go, too. Wherever it is that you go.'

'It doesn't work that way,' he says. 'There are rules.'

'There are always ways to get around the rules,' Miranda says. 'That was in another magazine.' She knows that she's babbling. A coping mechanism. There are articles about that, too. Why can't she stop thinking about women's magazines? Some byproduct of realizing that you're in love? 'Fifteen Ways to Know He Loves You Back.' Number eight. He doesn't object when you chain yourself to him after using fake snow in a magic spell to lure him into your arms.

The fake snow is colder and wetter and heavier than she'd thought it would be. Much more like real snow. Fenny has been muttering something against her neck. Either *I love you* or else *What the hell were you thinking, Miranda?*

It's both. He's saying both. It's fake snow and *real*. Real snow mingling with the fake. Her fake magic and real magic. Coming down heavier and heavier until all the world is white. The air, colder and colder and colder still.

'Something's happening, Fenny,' she says. 'It's snowing. Really snowing.'

It's as if he's turned to stone in her arms. She can feel him stop breathing. But his heart is racing. 'Let me go,' he says. 'Please let me go.'

'I can't,' Miranda says. 'I don't have the key.'

'You can.' A voice like a bell, clear and sweet.

And here is the one Miranda has been waiting for. Fenny's *she*. The one who catches foxes in traps. Never lets them go. The one who makes the rules.

It's silly, perhaps, to be reminded in this moment of Elspeth, but that's who Miranda thinks of when she looks up and sees the Lady who approaches, more Honeywell than any Honeywell Miranda has ever met. The presence, the *puissance* that Elspeth commands, just for a little while when Elspeth takes the stage, is a game. Elspeth plays at the thing. Here is the substance. Power is something granted willingly to Elspeth by her audience. Fenny's Lady has it always. What a burden. Never to be able to put it down.

Can the Lady see what Miranda is thinking? Her gaze takes in all. Fenny keeps his head bowed. But his hands are in Miranda's hands. He is in her keeping, and she will not let him go.

'I have no key,' Miranda says. 'And he does not want to go with you.'

'He did once,' the Lady says. She wears armor, too, all made of ice. What a thing it would be, to dress this Lady. To serve her. She could go with Fenny, if the Lady let her.

Down inside the dress where the Lady cannot see, Fenny pinches the soft web between Miranda's thumb and first finger. The pain brings her back to herself. She sees that he is watching her. He says nothing, only looks until Miranda finds herself again in his eyes.

'I went with you willingly,' Fenny agrees. But he doesn't look at the Lady. He only looks at Miranda.

'But you would leave me now? Only speak it and I will let you go at once.'

Fenny says nothing. A rule, Miranda thinks. There is a rule here. 'He can't say it,' she says. 'Because you won't let him. So let me say it for him. He will stay here. Haven't you kept him from his home for long enough?'

'His home is with me. Let him go,' the Lady says. 'Or you will be sorry.' She reaches out a long hand and touches the chain around Miranda's dress. It splinters beneath her feather-light touch. Miranda feels it give.

'Let him go and I will give you your heart's desire,' the

Lady says. She is so close that Miranda can feel the Lady's breath frosting her cheek. And then Miranda isn't holding Fenny. She's holding Daniel. Miranda and Daniel are married. They love each other so much. Honeywell Hall is her home. It always has been. Their children under the tree, Elspeth white-haired and lovely at the head of the table, wearing a dress from Miranda's couture label.

Only it isn't Elspeth at all, is it? It's the Lady. Miranda almost lets go of Daniel. Fenny! But he holds her hands and she wraps her hands around his waist, tighter than before.

'Be careful, girl,' the Lady says. 'He bites.'

Miranda is holding a fox. Scrabbling, snapping, blood breath at her face. Miranda holds fast.

Then: Fenny again. Trembling against her. 'It's okay,' Miranda says. 'I've got you.'

But it isn't Fenny after all. It's her mother. They're together in a small, dirty cell. Joannie says, 'It's okay, Miranda. I'm here. It's okay. You can let go. I'm here. Let go and we can go home.'

'No,' Miranda says, suddenly boiling with rage. 'No, you're not here. And I can't do anything about that. But I can do something about this.' And she holds on to her mother until her mother is Fenny again, and the Lady is looking at Miranda and Fenny as if they are a speck of filth beneath her slippered foot.

'Very well then,' the Lady says. She smiles, the way you would smile at a speck of filth. 'Keep him then. For a while. But know that he will never again know the joy that I taught him. With me he could not be but happy. I made him so. You will bring him grief and death. You have dragged him into a world where he knows nothing. Has nothing. He will look at you and think of what he lost.'

'We all lose,' says an acerbic voice. 'We all love and we all lose and we go on loving just the same.'

'Elspeth?' Miranda says. But she thinks, it's a trap. Just another trap. She squeezes Fenny so hard around his middle that he gasps.

Elspeth looks at Fenny. She says, 'I saw you once, I think. Outside the window. I thought you were a shadow or a ghost.'

Fenny says, 'I remember. Though you had hardly come into your beauty then.'

'Such talk! You are going to be wasted on my Miranda, I'm afraid,' Elspeth says. 'She's more for the doing of things than for the telling of them. As for you, my lady, I think you'll find you've been bested. Go and find another toy. We here are not your meat.'

The Lady curtseys. Looks one last time at Elspeth, Miranda. Fenny. This time he looks back. What does he see? Does any part of him move to follow her? His hand finds Miranda's hand again.

Then the Lady is gone and the snow thins and blows away to nothing at all.

Elspeth blows out a breath. 'Well,' she says. 'You're a stubborn girl, a good-hearted girl, Miranda, and brighter than your poor mother. But if I'd known what you were about, we would have had a word or two. Stage magic is well and good, but better to steer clear of the real kind.'

'Better for Miranda,' Fenny says. 'But she has won me free with her brave trick.'

'And now I suppose we'll have to figure out what to do with you,' Elspeth says. 'You'll be needing something more practical than that coat.'

'Come on,' Miranda says. She is still holding on to Fenny's hand. Perhaps she's holding on too tightly, but he doesn't seem to care. He's holding on just as tightly.

So she says, 'Let's go in.'

Acknowledgements

'The Visiting Star' by Robert Aickman © The Estate of Robert Aickman. 'Dinner For One' by Jenn Ashworth, first published in *Poor Souls' Light: Seven Curious Tales* (Curious Tales, 2014), is reprinted by permission of the author. 'This Beautiful House' from *Notwithstanding: Stories from an English Village* by Louis de Bernières, published by Vintage. First published in *The Times*, 2004. Copyright © Louis de Bernières 2004. Reproduced by permission of Felicity Bryan Literary Agency and the author. 'Nicholas Was' from Drabble II: Double Century by Neil Gaiman © copyright 1990 by Neil Gaiman. 'Someone in the Lift' by L. P. Hartley reproduced by kind permission of The Society of Authors as the Literary Representative of the Estate of L. P. Hartley. 'The Lady and the Fox' copyright © 2014 by Kelly Link first appeared in *My True Love Gave to Me*, edited by Stephanie Perkins (St. Martin's Press; 2014). Used by permission of the author. 'The Leaf-Sweeper' by Muriel Spark published in *The Complete Short Stories* by Canongate, reproduced by kind permission.

Every reasonable effort has been made to trace copyright holders, but if there are any errors or omissions, John Murray will be pleased to insert the appropriate acknowledgement in any subsequent printings or editions.